"There is no us, and there never will be again."

"Don't say that before you hear me out."

"You can't possibly have anything to say that will change my mind."

Nigel stepped around the counter, and before she knew what he was about to do, he had pulled her into his arms and was kissing her.

Startled by what was happening, Regina was momentarily unclear on how to react. Her thoughts flew out of her mind.

Something about being in the curve of those arms was familiar—the firmness of the grip about her waist, the abandon of the lips moving over hers, the heat rising between them. But everything else seemed part of the newness of him—the way his height sent her head back, the buttons of his suit pressing against her abdomen, the boldness of his fingers along her back, sparking flames in her.

These filled her senses, and she became lost in them.

Wait. What was she doing?

Startling her again, he pulled away.

Books by Yasmin Sullivan

Harlequin Kimani Romance

Return to Love

YASMIN SULLIVAN

grew up in upstate New York and St. Thomas, Virgin Islands, from which her family hails. She earned degrees from Howard University and Yale University. She currently lives in Washington, D.C., where she teaches with a focus on African-American and Caribbean literatures. When she isn't teaching, she does creative writing and works on mosaics.

Return to LOVE

YASMIN SULLIVAN

HARLEQUIN®

entertain, enrich, inspire™

For my mother, father, brother and grandmother,
who have given me the richness of the human heart;
for Jennie and Tanya,
who have been my sister-friends;
and for Madeline, Freddie and William,
who have shaped my vision of love.

ISBN-13: 978-0-373-86288-7

RETURN TO LOVE

Copyright © 2013 by Yasmin Y. DeGout

Recycling programs
for this product may
not exist in your area.

For questions and comments about the quality of this book, please contact us at CustomerService@Harlequin.com.

www.Harlequin.com

Printed in U.S.A.

Dear Kindred Spirit,

When characters interact across the pages of romance novels, they help us believe in the potential magic within our own lives. We are kindred spirits because we yearn for such journeys and open our hearts to transformation, greeting each other across the space of once blank lines.

I hope that this novel takes you on such a voyage and allows you to believe in the promise of second chances and the idea(l) that love can triumph over heartache. It is the story of Regina Gibson and Nigel Johns. Their young love ended in anguish, but their new risk might heal that void. I am grateful that you have decided to travel their story with me.

I am already working on my next romance project, and your comments on our journey here would be invaluable. I would love to hear from you at yasminhu@aol.com.

Warm wishes,

Yasmin

Chapter 1

When Regina Gibson heard the door swing open and the chime sound, she didn't glance up from the last shards of cobalt-blue tile she was fitting into place. She had them laid out in her mind, and if she looked away, the order would be lost.

She caught the coattails of a suit out of the corner of her eye and hoped he would be a paying customer.

"Let me know if you see anything," she called from the back.

It was getting on in the evening, but with the nearby restaurants still open, people wandered in now and again— once they could tell that the beaten-down corner house was now actually an art gallery and studio.

The exterior of the building hadn't been changed yet, except for a sign, but inside, they'd added installations, shelving, display cases, work spaces. They'd even added tables in the back rooms to teach classes, and they'd partitioned off the kilns.

Once the inside was in better shape, they could start work on the outside so that it didn't look like a rickety brownstone. And once they caught on, they could start the real renovations. It wasn't the perfect place yet, but it was the perfect location—right on the border of the arts and crafts district and near the Torpedo Factory Arts Center in Alexandria, Virginia.

Regina finished laying in the final pieces and cocked her head toward the back room, checking on the two kids. Kyle and Tenisha were still fixated on their little art projects. No problem there.

When she finally looked up, he was standing right in front of the table she was working at, his eyes trained on the children in the back room.

Her eyes didn't follow his gaze to the children. They were drawn to the figure in front of her. His rugged features seemed trapped and contained by his flawless business attire, but his athletic-cut suit didn't hide the rough-hewn inflections or the ridged sculpting of his body. The polish of the crisp navy cotton didn't conceal a raw, unrefined beauty in his shape. It was as if something untamed was tamped down by the elegance of professional trappings.

He had a firm, never-back-down stance that said he would be a hard adversary to rumble with in…whatever his business was. And it was business. Everything about him said that he was all business—everything from the no-nonsense cut of his suit to the angular inlay of his jawline. The smooth, dark brown skin of his face held a concentrated expression that was softened but made no less determined by the curves of thick, sensuous lips. His eyes were serious but also wistful. His eyes…

Regina flinched and sucked in a breath. She knew those eyes.

The face was older, harder, different than the face she had known before. But inside it was the prior face, and she recognized it now as if someone had just pointed it out to her. The childhood had gone out of it—the baby fat that had plumped his cheeks, the boyish grin that made his eyes sparkle. These had been replaced by the calm, jagged confidence of an adult. He would be twenty-eight now—the same as her. He even seemed taller, his shoulders broader.

Regina could barely place this new configuration with what she knew of the boy behind it. It didn't fit the idler she had known—the slacker lazing on the sofa with his buddies or running the streets with his jeans hanging halfway down his hips. The face before her didn't match the one she had known, the one skipping classes and sleeping through exams. The one who had skipped out on her.

As recognition dawned, so did Regina's rage.

What made him think he could pop in on her after all this time? No way. No how.

Growing more livid with each second, Regina shoved the plywood base of her mosaic farther onto the table, got up from her chair and walked over to the display case on which the cash register sat. This put them out of sight and out of earshot of the children.

Nigel Johns had understood to follow her across the room and now faced her across the counter. And what she faced was wrath.

"Unless you know how to turn back time or are here to tell me I've won the lottery, you better get the hell out."

Regina's voice was low, but its venom was unmistakable, and her body clenched in outrage.

His eyes now turned to her for the first time, but what she found there she couldn't decipher.

"I'm not here for any of that. I'm here for you and—"

"You're not here for me or anything else, because I don't want to have anything to do with you."

His face remained calm, and his tone remained even and commanding, which infuriated her more. He may have thought he could waltz in the door, but she would be cutting him off at every pass.

As if it would somehow explain things, he took a folded sheet of paper out of his pocket and put it down on the counter.

"This is for you—for—"

"Whatever it is, I don't want it."

When he didn't move, she snatched up the sheet of paper and unfolded it. It was a check for five thousand dollars.

"You think you can buy me?" she said, ripping up the check. "You think you have anything that I want?" She threw the pieces at his fine navy suit and watched them scatter down to the floor. "I told you before, didn't I? I don't need you. Now get the hell out."

Nigel Johns held his stance. Maybe he was waiting for her to get it off her chest and get it over with. But it wouldn't be over anytime soon.

Regina put her hands on her hips and simply glared at him. He said nothing, but he also didn't move.

"Wait," she said. "Do you have a card? I have an item that belongs to you—to your grandmother, actually—and once you have it back, I won't need to hear from you ever again."

He sighed heavily.

"This is not the way I wanted this to be, Reggie."

His voice was low, but it was deep and steady. Even that had changed. The disappointment in his tone calmed her a bit, but her position had not altered, and she held her ground.

"This is not the way it's supposed to be between us," he said.

Regina couldn't believe his audacity. Were they on the same planet? She hadn't seen him in over six years!

She threw her hands up in exasperation.

"There is no us, and there never will be again."

"Don't say that before you hear me out."

"You can't possibly have anything to say that will change my mind."

Nigel stepped around the counter, and before she knew what he was about to do, he had pulled her into his arms and was kissing her.

Startled by what was happening, Regina was momentarily unclear on how to react. Her thoughts flew out of her mind.

Something about being in the curve of these arms was familiar—the firmness of the grip about her waist, the abandon of the lips moving over hers, the heat rising up between them. But everything else seemed part of the newness of him—the way his height sent her head back, the buttons of his suit pressing against her abdomen, the boldness of his fingers along her back, sparking flames in her.

These filled her senses, and she became lost in them.

Wait. What was she doing?

Startling her again, he pulled away.

"That's the way it always was for us," he said, letting her go and stepping back.

Regina felt like she'd been caught in a lie, one he'd forced her to tell, and her anger sprang back to life. How could she let herself get caught in the moment? And how dare he put his hands on her after he had disappeared—ditching her, ditching them, ditching everything?

No way was it going to go down like that.

She stepped up to him, poking her finger against his chest and raising her head for the attack. But she didn't know what to say. Her head had not cleared; she hadn't been able to remember her logical arguments about why what had just happened didn't change anything.

Little footsteps clacked toward the front, and both of them stopped in their tracks.

Tenisha appeared, smocked in the jumbo trash bag that Regina had tied at her neck and around her waist. And thank goodness. The bag was covered from top to bottom with splotches of paint, swipes from the brushes and handprints of various sizes.

Tenisha hesitated when she saw a man there.

"Come, sweetie. What is it?" Regina coaxed, giving her full attention to the child and relieved to have a moment to collect her thoughts.

Nigel stepped back around the counter, his eyes fixed on the little girl.

Behind Tenisha trailed a path of paint that was dripping from the ceramic bisque platter she was carrying. It was shaped like a butterfly, its various quadrants plastered with pastel shades of glaze.

"I'm finished with mine. Kyle is still working on his."

"Did you get the bottom, honey?"

"Yup. Look."

She turned it over for Regina to inspect, all the while smudging little fingerprints of paint from one color to another.

Regina took her back to the table in the classroom.

"Let's just set it here to dry for a few minutes before we add a topcoat." She turned to the little boy, still vigorously applying paint to the baseball-shaped bisque platter he was working on. "How is yours going, little one?"

"Uh-huh."

Regina could see that Kyle was fully engrossed, and so she turned back to Tenisha.

"Once we add the topcoat, we can put these in the kiln and head upstairs to have something to eat. Okay?"

"Okay."

"You sit here and keep Kyle company while he finishes his. Is that okay?"

"Okay."

Regina turned and walked back to the register. Nigel had popped up thinking…whatever he was thinking, but it wasn't going to work on her.

"I've had enough, Nigel. There is no us, and there will be no us."

When the corners of his lips twisted into a smirk, Regina's temper stirred again, and she seethed. She'd wanted to be calm, but he wasn't going to let that happen.

"Get out. Get out, and don't come back here."

"Reggie, I—"

"No. Get out."

When the chime at the door sounded, neither one looked over.

"Get out," she said again.

Neither moved.

"Hey, hey. Is anything wrong here?"

Regina knew Jason's voice immediately and was relieved when he came over to stand next to her. He was over six feet four inches, and he worked out religiously. It was clear to all three that Nigel, despite his new height and weight, couldn't take Jason even if he tried. There was nothing left for him to do but withdraw.

Only he wasn't going to back down easily. He held his ground and gave a brief nod to the other man, as if sizing up his competition. Yes, he must be a formidable adversary in the business world.

"Nothing's wrong. This man is just leaving," said Regina.

Nigel didn't move right away, and when he did, it wasn't in the direction of the door. He casually searched one of his inner coat pockets and took out a silver case—a business-card holder.

"You asked if I have a card."

He took out one of the cards and stepped up to the register, handing it in her direction.

When Regina didn't move to take the card, he laid it on the counter. She glared at it as if it had leprosy and then glared at Nigel.

"I'll get that item out to you as soon as possible," she said in a professional tone, stifling her hostility.

Nigel bent his upper body toward her.

"This isn't over, Reggie."

She picked up the business card and put it in the pocket of her jeans.

"It will be soon enough."

Regina watched as Nigel slowly walked out of the studio. She was completely shaken.

Jason, holding Kyle on his hip, sat down at the workstation in the back of the shop.

"You need to talk?"

"No. Yes."

Regina walked over to the table, glancing in on Tenisha before sitting down. Tenisha was blowing on her plate to get it to dry, and Kyle squirmed down to go get his piece.

"It can wait until tomorrow."

"I got time now."

"No. Really. It will be better said tomorrow."

Kyle returned with his baseball platter. "I made this for you, Daddy."

"I can scc that you did."

Jason smiled down at his son and took the plate from him before lifting him back onto his lap.

"Here," said Regina. "Let me have the platter so that I can topcoat it and get it in the kiln."

"But I made it for Daddy."

"I know, sweetie, but it's not finished yet. We want it to be hard on the outside so that you can use it. Come, let me show you."

Regina was almost finished applying the topcoat when the bell at the door chimed. He wouldn't have come back, would he? How dare he show up out of nowhere—twice?

Luckily, it was only Ellison, who had come to look for his partner and child.

"Hey. What's the deal with leaving me in the car?"

"My bad. We're in here," Jason called to him. "The pieces aren't done yet. You want to wait or come back another time?"

Before he could answer, Regina offered, "I have some lasagna upstairs. You can eat while you wait for the kiln to fire them."

"We can wait," Ellison replied, picking up Kyle.

Regina set the cones and started filling the kiln. Nigel had had the nerve to throw money at her like she could be bought.

"It's set. Let's lock the front door and head out back."

Gathering Tenisha in her arms, she climbed up the back stairs and let her down to unlock the apartment. She was glad for the company but couldn't keep her mind focused on the random conversations that popped up between them.

Keeping her hands busy wasn't a problem. She heated up and dished out the lasagna, got them all soda and bread, got the adults salad, found an animated movie that the kids could watch and ran down to check on the kiln.

Quieting her mind was another story. What had happened when he'd started to kiss her? Why hadn't she thought to push him off right away? It was because she hadn't known what he was going to do. But that would not happen again.

She heard a car pull up out back, and her pulse quickened. But it was only Tenisha's mom, as expected. *Get a grip, girl. He won't have the nerve to just show up again anytime soon, and if he does, I'll be ready for him.*

While Jason opened the door, Regina moved into the kitchen to fix another plate of lasagna. She stopped and pulled out the business card from her pocket. It was a local address. Damn.

That was okay. She had what she needed to send him the item. No use worrying about it now. In fact, she would be rid of him for good soon enough.

Chapter 2

"Get out. Get out, and don't come back here."

He knew the moment she opened her mouth that he shouldn't have gone. And though he'd taken his time leaving, it was clear that he'd been outgunned.

If he had any hope at all, it was that fraction of a second during his kiss when he felt her lips part beneath his, felt her body arch ever so slightly against his chest. But her arms never came around him, and then he saw the reason why.

He had heard the little boy call out "Daddy" and come running, wrapped in a paint-splattered garbage bag just like the little girl. It had gotten dark outside while he'd been there, so in the glass of the front door, he had been able to see over his shoulder. He could see the little boy jump into the man's arms, talking a mile a minute about whatever it was that he'd made.

He hadn't lost his stride, but his heart just about broke.

He never imagined that when he was ready, it would be too late.

"I don't need you. Now get the hell out."

Inwardly, he was shaking his head. Her hair had been longer, but still smooth and shiny, and her almond eyes had been as piercing as ever. She had been as beautiful and as sensuous as the day she had driven him away, and things could not have gone more badly.

Nigel Johns sat behind his mahogany desk with spreadsheets piled up on his right and a keyboard in front of him. Today, he was off his game. This wasn't like him, and it wasn't good.

He worked in the accounting department of an investing and accounting firm. He hadn't been there very long, but he was doing well, thanks to what he was able to do for his clients and what he'd done with his own portfolio.

"We don't need you, so just leave, and don't come back."

He hadn't expected her to fall into his arms, but he'd thought they could talk like two rational adults—now that he was an adult. But that was admitting that he hadn't been before. Well, it was true, he hadn't been. Their breakup had been his fault, and now maybe it was too late.

He'd decided to crunch numbers for the rest of the day—something simple he could do without too much thought. He always double-checked every calculation, but today he was having to triple and quadruple check because his mind just wasn't where it should be.

"I don't need you. Now get the hell out."

He should have sent her the money, laid out a plan and put the plan fully into place before entering the picture himself. If he hadn't gone there...

He wasn't getting much done. He pushed the keyboard away, shaking his head. He had clients coming in within the hour. At least their folders were ready, and the review of the accounting figures would be easy. This was a good thing, because where his head was right now didn't leave him a great deal of concentration.

"...so just leave, and don't come back."

He'd allowed himself to be chased off once. It was the last time that they'd seen each other six years ago. It was in college, and he was in her apartment. They'd been arguing more, but he didn't expect her to actually call their wedding off and cast him to the wind. She'd used the same kind of language.

"Now get the hell out."

No way was he going to be run off again. If he hadn't gone there, things might have worked out differently. But in for a penny, in for a pound. Now that he'd shown himself, he wasn't backing down, and she wasn't keeping him from his child.

Children? Was it one, or was it both of them? The girl was bigger, but then girls grew faster. Right? He wasn't sure, but he sure as hell was going to find out.

He'd only found out a few months ago that there was a child—or children. He'd been working, saving, building a life that he could offer Regina. He didn't want her to see him until he had made it—made something of himself that contradicted the waste of time he'd been in college. The news had hit him square in the gut.

"You ever see Regina? You been in touch with her since then?"

He was visiting his parents at home when he'd run into one of his college buddies—the one who used to date Regina's roommate. The question put him on guard because it pried into places he didn't want opened.

"Why do you ask?"

He wanted to skirt the issue and let it die, but his friend persisted.

"Because I need to know if you ever found out."

"Found out what?"

The silence and the cryptic way his friend was treading around the subject told him that whatever it was, it was serious.

"Found out what?"

"Look, I'm not supposed to know, but I've never stopped thinking that you should have known."

"Known what?"

"Regina was pregnant when she graduated."

"Pregnant?"

"She was pregnant, and it was yours, and that's all I know."

This was all the information he could get out of his old friend, but it sent him reeling.

Regina had called things off between them just before she graduated. They were supposed to graduate together from Howard University and then get married. Except that, by the end of senior year, he was still a year behind on his classes because he'd been partying too much.

His parents had never given up on him, even after his near-failing grade reports. When Regina put him out, he'd felt like nothing. He'd decided not to come back until he'd made something of himself, until he could show her that he could take care of things. Although he tried, he couldn't do much about that semester, and he mourned the whole summer over their breakup. But the following semester, after she'd already finished and moved on, he was back with a vengeance, determined to prove himself.

He finished his undergraduate degree in accounting and did an internship within the year. Then he went on to an MBA in accounting and finance. He couldn't get into an accelerated program because of his grade point average, but he used the two-year program to take real-estate and investment classes. He graduated at the top of his class and then sat for the CPA exam.

In a way, his goal had become money. He joined an accounting firm and used all his degrees to start amassing a bank account. Then he made a vertical move to the position he was in now so that he could move back to the DC area, where Regina still was.

But it wasn't just money; he wanted everything that came with real success, real responsibility. And he wanted to be more cultured, too. No more baggy pants, no more ghetto fashion, no more looking like the hood. Everything about his life was bent on making it, looking the part, being professional, working hard, getting it right.

She'd gone to study with some artists for a year—or so he'd heard. But other than that, she had stayed in the area after their Howard years. He didn't have many details; after a while people had finally started to get the message and had stopped telling him her activities. By the time she got back to DC after her year away, he was immersed in his own MBA program down home in South Carolina, trying to catch up. What his buddy had said fell into place. That year away would have been when she'd had their child.

Was it one child or two? Yes, he would be finding out.

He just had to get through the day. Then he had to get his game back and make it through the rest of the week. This weekend he would stake his claim.

Regina turned the car off and grabbed her purse. She'd had an errand to run for her morning office job, and then she had to drop off some of her pieces at a gallery downtown that was having a showing of local artists. By the time she got to the studio, she was running late.

She found Amelie finishing up with a customer. She had sold one of her large, bead-covered bowls and had a new beadwork project in process on the back table in the bead section.

"Sorry I'm late. I hope that means we've been doing well today."

"No problem, and yes—relatively speaking. We've sold one of yours and one of mine. Whoo-hoo."

There was no one else in the shop, so Regina started pulling out her project. "I don't know if that's anything to whoo-hoo about. But it's good. We have to get our front fixed up soon."

"I know. I registered us for the seminar you were talking about," Amelie said, "the one at the community center on starting up a small business."

"Oh, good. I've been working on our paperwork from the books I found."

And she had been. It was like having another part-time job. Regina pulled out her tiles and began setting up her workstation.

"I didn't make it to the post office today," Regina said.

"I'm going to leave early to get some of my jewelry to the consignment shop. Is there anything you want me to take to the post office for you on my way?"

"No, I haven't even wrapped the package yet. I'll get it tomorrow. You take off."

"Okay. I put out two new pieces. This one—" Amelie pointed to a necklace "—is made of yellow jasper beads with cowrie shell accents, and this one—" she pointed to a jewelry box "—is made with rose quartz and Czech glass."

"They're beautiful. You keep getting more elaborate."

"That's the point."

After Amelie left, Regina sat down to her project. She was on the sky section and needed to break some more light blue and white tiles. It was the act of hammering the pieces under a cloth that made her think of Nigel. That fraud.

She replaced the cloth and banged the center of a large blue tile, splitting it into triangles. It had been almost a week since he'd appeared out of the blue, and she'd finally stopped worrying that every stranger who turned up might be him coming back for round two.

She straightened out the cloth and went for the triangles, smashing them into small trapezoids. She would get him his item and be done with him. She had too much going on in her life that she wanted to get done. She didn't need one more thing to distract her.

Nigel checked the inside pocket of his sports suit to make sure he had everything. She wouldn't be flinging his check back at him this time. He took a breath. No need to go there yet. He hadn't gotten anything in the mail, so maybe her bark wasn't as bad as her bite.

He got out of the car and started unloading the packages from the backseat. It was after 8:00 p.m. on a Sunday, and the studio was closed, so he assumed they'd be home, tomorrow being a school day. He'd get all the packages up the back steps before ringing the buzzer.

It was beginning to get dark outside, so when she opened the door, the warm, yellow light from inside haloed behind her and made her look like an angel—his angel. She had on white leggings and a summer camisole, but the soft fabrics hugged her curves in a way that made his mouth water.

Except that her hips were deeper, she hadn't changed from the girl he loved. She had natural dimples in the curve of her cheeks so that she looked always on the verge of a smile, and her tapered waist flared out into the most lus-

Return to Love

cious behind he'd ever seen. Even in the simple leggings that she had on now, she made his knees weak.

Her hair was different this time—pulled back in a ponytail at the nape of her neck in a way that emphasized her umber eyes. The anger he saw form in her eyes at the sight of him in the doorway snapped him back to the present, to the fact that they were torn apart.

"Hello, Reggie."

"Don't hello me. What on earth are you doing at my house?"

The moment she opened her mouth, his calm was shattered, but he didn't show it. There was no mistaking the animosity in her voice. She didn't want him in her private space. She didn't want him anywhere near her at all.

"I still need to speak with you. Can I come in?"

"No. No, you cannot. And I don't have anything to say to you."

He didn't want to force things with her. He'd let her cut him off time and again in the studio, intentionally giving her the upper hand so that she could see that he wasn't there to threaten her. But this time, he wasn't going to back down. This time, he wasn't going to be sent away.

"Look, Reggie. You and whoever you're with will not keep me from my child. Or children. You don't have the right to do that."

"What?"

"I want to see my children. I know I haven't been there for them so far, but that will not be the case from here on out."

She sighed, and he saw some of the fight go out of her— not the rage or the anger that he saw in her eyes, but some of the fight. Her shoulders slumped, and she turned into the apartment, walking away from him.

He gathered up the packages from the stairwell and

followed her inside. She had her back to him and seemed to be staring at the wall or at nothing, so he shut the door behind them.

He had been gone a long time. He knew that. Perhaps she had to decide if he was safe or if she was willing to share their children. Or perhaps she just needed to get her mind accustomed to the idea.

He was standing in what turned out to be the dining area, with a kitchen off to the side. There was no partition separating it from the living room, where she now stood.

The first thing he saw was the art. It filled her rooms with color, and she'd even painted the chairs and cabinets and bookshelves to make them pop. All of her touches filled the room—the African masks and dolls on the walls, the embroidered cushions on the sofa, the framed paintings and mosaics covering the walls. So much claimed his eyes that he almost missed how worn down the permanent structure underneath was.

The kitchen and dining nook seemed to have come straight out of the '60s—battered wooden cabinets, ancient countertops, worn linoleum flooring—and the rest of the place didn't fare much better. Downstairs, everything that they'd added stood out as new against the old.

Her voice tore him away from his perusal.

"How did you find out?"

He put his bundles down.

"I found out from someone who's not supposed to know."

"Please tell me."

The resignation in her voice pulled at his heartstrings.

"I ran into your roommate's ex-boyfriend a few months ago. But it shouldn't have taken finding that out to make me come look for you. I just wanted to make something of myself before I did. But when I found out that you were

pregnant when…when you called things off between us…
Reggie, why didn't you tell me? Why did you send me
away without me knowing?"

He took a step toward her, but she took a step back.

"What would you have done? You were too busy hanging with your friends and blowing off school. You might
have stayed, but it would have been for the wrong reasons.
And I didn't need you to make a life for…"

She shook her head, trailing off.

"But I should have known. I had a right to know. And
if—"

"Let it go."

"Why didn't you tell me?"

Her jaw was set in a rigid line that told him she would
not be offering any answer to that question.

"Where are they, Reggie? I want to see them. And I
plan to be there for them from now on. It doesn't matter if
you're with someone else. I'm still their father."

He pulled the check out of his suit pocket.

"If you don't want it, that's fine. But they deserve it.
And so do you. Where are they?"

She looked at him as he put the check down on the dining table, and what he saw in her wet eyes was a combina-
tion of sadness and hate.

She turned away from him again and buried her face
in her hands. When she spoke, it was through tears, but
it was with rage.

"There is no they."

He didn't understand. "What?"

"Don't you get it? There is no they. There was no child."

He wondered for a split second if she had…let go of
it…after they had broken apart. But then he looked at her
shaking shoulders. He knew her better than to think that.

"No child?"

It started to sink in. He wasn't a father. The little boy he had seen wasn't his. Nor the little girl. His child had not made it. His heart fell. He crossed over to her but stopped just behind her without touching her, not knowing how to comfort her, not knowing if she would receive his comfort.

"There was no child," she said again, stammering. She whirled toward him, ready to strike, but didn't. She just stopped and stared at his face, her own face crumpling.

He wrapped his arms around her shoulders and drew her to him, but she wrangled against him.

"There was no child," she repeated, lashing at his chest with her fists. It was like a dam had broken, as though she couldn't stop herself once she'd started letting it out. She kept pummeling his chest with her fists as if it was his fault, or maybe because he'd been the one to make her say it, relive it. "And you weren't there."

She drew back after she said it—the truth of it all. She had tears spilling down her face, and her fists were still balled, ready to strike. Her eyes were red and wet, filled with rage and hate. And now he knew why.

Regina kept hammering at him, as if she wanted to pound him until all the hurt she had carried over the years was finally over. But when she stood back and looked up at his face, what she saw there stopped her. Nigel wondered if she could see that the disappointment in his eyes was as bottomless as her own heartbreak must have been. Nigel knew the moment that the resistance went out of her and stepped toward her, folding her in his arms again.

"When I saw the kids downstairs—"

He wanted to go on, but he couldn't control his voice.

For a while she didn't say anything but simply sobbed against his chest.

When she found her voice, it was shaky. "I was babysitting. Kyle belongs to Jason, and Tenisha to another friend.

They're not related, and they're not even the same age. Kyle is five and a half, and Tenisha is seven."

After she got the words out, she convulsed in tears again.

He just held her while she wept.

When he thought she was back in control, he ventured, "What happened...to ours?"

For a few moments, she cried harder. Then she took in a deep breath.

"I lost it. I miscarried."

She broke from him and went to the window, trying to wipe her face with her hands.

"And guess when. Guess."

Her tone was sardonic, but she was still fighting back her tears.

"On the day that would have been our wedding day," she said.

He went to her and wrapped his arms around her again, but she fought him. "No. You weren't there. You weren't there."

She hit at his shoulders with her open palms, her body racked by sobs.

He pulled her into his embrace. "I'm so sorry," he said into her hair. "I'm so sorry. Please forgive me."

"No. I won't."

"Please. I didn't know."

"You should have known. You should have been there."

"You sent me away, Reggie."

She was silent, tears still streaming down her face. He held her and rubbed her back until her body shook less. He smoothed her hair and kissed her temples until her tears abated some. He ignored her periodic attempts to rustle from his arms.

When she had stilled, he pulled her chin up to look at

her, to see that she was all right. Her eyes were red from crying, and her lips were tender from being pressed so hard together. He wanted to drain the redness from her eyes and soothe the pain out of her expression.

"I'm so sorry, Reggie, so sorry."

He folded her against his chest and ran his hand down her back. In the quiet, he could feel the way her body pressed against his in the embrace. He wanted to feel that forever. He wanted to make her his again.

This time when he pulled her face up to his, he bent down, softly kissing her lips. He wanted to turn back time, to undo the hurt he'd caused, to be there when he should have been there.

"I'm so sorry, baby."

She said nothing, but she didn't move from his arms either.

He bent his head to the side of her face and kissed her eyelid, her cheek, her earlobe. Then he cupped her head and took her mouth with his, parting her lips with his own and claiming her breath.

He felt her hands tighten around his upper arms and knew that her body was responding. He wanted to assuage the hurt inside her with his lips, pacify the anger out of her with his fingertips.

When he moved his tongue into her mouth, it opened for him, and a quiet murmur escaped into his mouth, igniting fire inside of him. She took a small step back, but he stepped with her, closing the gap between them before she could make it. He claimed her hips with his hands and pressed her against his loins. She sucked in her breath and then another murmur filled his mouth.

She put her arms around his neck, and her tongue played against his, inviting him deeper inside. He could read her desire. He had always been able to. It was clear that she was starting to want him the way he wanted her.

Nigel could sense the battle being waged inside Regina. The years of hurt and anger, of bearing the burden alone, were at odds with everything else that was happening between them. He wanted for everything else to win.

"Let me be there for you now," he whispered against her lips.

Then he reclaimed her mouth, running his hands along her back. He couldn't resist cupping her bottom and pulling her closer, and when he did, he felt a slight tilt of her hips as she drew nearer. He knew where she yearned, and he wanted to ease that need, even as his own grew hotter and less controllable with every passing minute.

He bent down farther, his mouth finding her neck, and cupped her buttocks again, lifting her body against his. When he heard her low moan against his ear, he lifted her off her feet and strode toward the back of the apartment to find her bedroom.

He expected her to stop him, but she said nothing while he eased her down on the bed and lowered himself over her, pressing his swollen groin against her sweet center. Instead, she reached for his arms and pulled him closer to her, kneading herself along his body. It had been so long for him that even this small movement sent him close to the edge, but he knew better than to let himself go. He knew that this was for her, that this was to let her know that she wasn't alone all that time, that he was still loving her. It was to calm the sore places, to hush the anger and the rage.

He looked at her tearstained face in the moonlight. He had been waiting for this for so long, so long. Her fingers at his back let him know that his wait would soon be over. But he wouldn't rush to that place. This was for her.

He settled next to her and slid his hand into her leggings.

When he found the wetness of her womanhood, his loins leapt, and he heard her moan.

Her long, sepia legs came into view as he removed her leggings, and her beautiful breasts fell into the open as he pulled the camisole over her head and undid her bra. He pulled the bow from her hair and laid her back down. He meant to take his own clothes off as well, but the sight of her pulled him back to the bed.

When he took the closest breast into his mouth, he heard her moan. He couldn't resist the feel of her nipple against his tongue, the feel of her wetness at his fingertips, the way her body writhed with his caresses. This was for her.

Before he lost control, he stood up and removed his suit, his shirt, the rest of his clothes. He found a condom and got it on quickly, returning to Regina's side on the bedspread. He kissed her, reminding himself to take it slowly. This was for her.

He ran his hand over her body, listening for the places that made her breath heavy and feeling for the places that made her body sway toward his. He kissed her neck and pulled her leg over his thigh so that he could touch her warm, wet center again, and when he did, she let out a low, guttural moan that filled his body with need. He couldn't wait any longer.

When he moved between her thighs, her legs spread for him, pressing against his hips. And when he entered her, her mouth opened beneath his, drawing him in. He pressed gently toward her center, stifling his own moan and barely able to keep control. It had always been this way for him with this woman.

She moaned as he pressed slowly inside of her. She was as tight as she had been the first time they had been together many years ago, tighter even than he remembered. Drowning in her beauty, he found her mouth and covered it again with his own. He had to remind himself to slow down, to take his time. He had been wanting this for so long, so long. But this was for her.

Chapter 3

Regina got up before the sun came up. The bed next to her was empty, but she had been wrapped in the top sheet and spread. Her body was still pleasantly tender from the activity of the night before, and she was glad to have some time to collect her thoughts before beginning her day. Even more so, she was glad to have time before facing Nigel again—time to figure out what to say, how to explain that things had gotten out of hand.

She knew she should have stopped him when he kissed her, but after the emotional roller coaster of the evening—the anger that he had come back again, the anguish over the fresh memory of the loss of their child, the unspeakable shame that she had lost it—after all of that, she needed those arms around her.

When she had looked in his face, she had finally seen someone who understood what having and then losing their child had meant to her. And for the first time, she had just let herself cry.

Someone could finally comprehend what she had been through, someone who felt the pain, as well. Maybe that was what had wrenched all of that turmoil to the top. Maybe that was what had made her vulnerable to his advances.

She should have stopped him when he ran his hand up and down her back, sending tingles through her, but right then, the wounds in her had finally found a place where they could be held, and she wasn't willing to leave that shelter. She hadn't been touched in so long. She hadn't had a place to unburden the past. That's what his hands did to her. They softened the rage; they caressed the hurt.

She should have stopped him when he carried her to her bedroom, but she hadn't been touched with understanding in so long—the kind of understanding that made her needy and wanting. Yes, by then, she wanted it as much as he did.

She should have stopped him, but it had always been this way between them.

Regina kicked off the sheets and went into the bathroom to run a bath. It wasn't her usual routine, but she had time, and it would help her calm down and think.

He was taller than he'd been before, but mostly, he was more in control, more able to take his time, more able to respond to her body rather than running along ahead of her. This made him a different lover than the one she had known.

Having him inside of her had felt just like the first time. He was slow and gentle. He filled her with his presence. At first, he had made long, slow thrusts, stroking the aches out of her and making her body arch off the bed. Then he had found her spots and made her eager, pushed her toward the edge.

He had kissed her tears, lulling her sadness away, consoling her heartbreak. But he had also run his thumbs over her breasts, lighting fire in her. Between the tenderness and the flame, she wasn't sure which was most consuming, most arousing.

When he cupped her head in his palms and kissed her, the gentleness of his kiss had alleviated her anger and healed her bruises, but his chest moving along her breasts as he plunged inside of her made her wrap her legs around him and draw him farther inside.

"Reggie, Reggie, I've missed you so much," he had murmured over and over.

His deep voice sent tingles down her back, and when he whispered it against her ear, her body had broken out in goose bumps, and an agonizing pressure built up at her center.

"Tell me what you need, baby," he had said.

She couldn't speak, and she just held on, clinging to his shoulders. She only needed.

Then he had moved his hand down between them and begun to massage her while he moved inside of her, making her moan, making her grind against him, tears streaming from the corners of her eyes. Then the first waves of climax hit her, and her body gripped his length. He groaned and thrust against her, but waited for her full release before burying his face next to hers and bucking inside of her as he rode his own wave of orgasm. When it was over, she had turned from him, and he had pulled her back against his chest, and they had slept spooned together that way.

Remembering the night sent arrows of heat through Regina's body. She was letting the memory overwhelm her, when she needed to be figuring out what to do now and where they would go from here.

Only, there was no they, and one night of passion didn't erase six years of frustration and hurt and loneliness. It didn't bring back their child or make their wedding happen. It didn't turn back time.

Nigel had woken up early, before dawn. He couldn't get back to sleep, but he didn't want to wake up Regina. He thought about it—round two—but decided he had better not. His day would have to start in a bit, and he wouldn't be able to take his time.

He just held her for a while, smiling to himself because she was back in his arms. His happiness was tainted by the fact that their child had been lost. He still needed to deal with that, and he needed to help Regina deal with it, too. He could see how much she was still hurting, and how angry she was that he hadn't been there. He could never make up for that, but he wanted to spend the rest of his life trying.

Nigel slipped out of bed just as the sun was about to come up. He washed up as best he could, dressed and went to look for something for them to eat. He didn't know whether she had to be up early on a Monday or what time the studio opened, but he knew he would wake her before he left. This way, they could have breakfast together. They could start their day and their lives together, start healing.

He found her key on the counter next to her purse and drove down the street to see if any place was open. It turned out that he could have walked, because the café on the corner already had customers. He got them bagels with cream cheese, bacon and eggs, pancakes, orange juice and coffee—more than they could eat.

When he got back, he heard her running water in the bathroom but decided not to disturb her just yet. He found a fork and sat down to his breakfast, checking out her pieces on the walls and thinking about where each one could go when they had their own place.

Nigel caught himself imagining their life together and sighed. They had a lot of talking and healing and forgiving left to do, but he was eager to begin the journey.

Regina didn't smell the bacon until she was almost finished getting dressed. Was he still there? She threw on some slacks and a top and peeked out of her bedroom.

He smiled at her from the dining table and began moving the packages he had brought the night before to clear a space for her to sit. His smile almost turned his face into the boyish one she had known before—almost. The cheeks plumped out the way they used to, but the rougher angles remained.

"I thought I smelled bacon..."

"Good morning, beautiful. You did."

"...but I knew I didn't have bacon in the house."

"No, I ran down to the corner to get us something. I hope you're hungry because I think I overdid it. Come sit."

Before she could sit down, he pulled her onto his lap and into a long hug. He kissed her cheek and her forehead. He didn't seem to notice that her body stiffened now at this touch. And before she could protest to the affection, he released her to the chair he had cleared.

She could tell that they weren't on the same page about last night. She wasn't ready to broach the issue, but she knew she had to.

"I thought you were gone," she said.

He must have read that hesitance in her voice as concern or disappointment because he slid his hand under her chin to pull her face toward his. He caressed her cheek with his thumb and said, "No, no way. You must think I'm a rat."

He let her face go and uncovered her plate and juice,

smiling at her. "I know I have a lot to make up for, a lot to prove, but I won't be running out ever again. I just went to get us some eats. I figured we needed it after last night, which was…amazing."

Regina looked at the mound of food in front of her and tried to figure out how to get them on the same page.

"I got up early and didn't want to wake you. I didn't know what time you had to be up."

"Early."

"Then eat up."

Regina heard the mirth in Nigel's tone when he mentioned last night. She read the possessiveness in Nigel's eyes when he looked at her. In contrast, she couldn't even bring herself to eat. Tired of pushing the food around on the plate, she put the fork down and just looked at it, trying to find the right words.

He came around the table and knelt down next to her chair.

"Hey, what's wrong, Reggie? I know there's hurt, but we'll face that together now." He put his arms around her and pulled her toward his chest. Regina tensed, not responding to the embrace.

"Hey, what's wrong?"

"I think we need to talk."

Nigel scooted back onto his chair. He bent toward her and covered her hand with his own. "Okay. What's going on?"

"Last night was…"

She saw his face drop, as if he could tell what was coming.

"…like it used to be between us."

"But?"

"But it's just what it was."

"Which is?"

"Something we both needed."

He let go of her hand and leaned back in his chair.

"That's not all it was, Reggie. Don't you know that?"

His voice was calm and sincere, but it had an edge that bordered on exasperation. His eyes pleaded with her to see it his way.

"That's all it can be. I don't even know you anymore."

"But that's what I want, Reggie—for us to spend the time getting to know one another again. You don't have to make any decisions now. Just give it a chance."

Regina got up and covered her plate before taking it to the fridge. She needed to be away from his eyes for a minute, to have something to do with her hands. His eyes followed her every move.

"No. We had a chance. I can't go back there. Maybe I'm just finally getting over what happened back then."

"Maybe I am, too. Maybe it's something we can do together."

She whirled around and looked right at him. "I can't just forgive you for leaving and then for not being there when I needed you."

He balled his fists and shook his head. They had finally gotten to the real issue.

"You told me to leave. You put me out. You can't put me out and then hold it against me when I go. And you didn't tell me about...the baby."

"We were engaged. I needed you to be more serious about life, especially about our life together. You weren't supposed to jump ship. You were supposed to grow up. You should have been there."

"How can—"

"Stop. I'm not going to argue with you. And that's all we can do now because we're never going to agree on it."

Regina got up from the table. This wasn't going well. They were never going to see eye to eye. She disappeared into the bedroom and returned with a small, black jewelry case.

"Here."

She handed him the case, and he opened it. It was his grandmother's wedding ring.

"I'm sorry I didn't have time to mail it."

"It wasn't just time. If it was that important, you would have mailed it. There's a reason you didn't make the time to do it."

She considered his statement. Maybe it was true. Maybe she'd dawdled because part of her wanted to keep the past alive, to have a keepsake of it.

"Maybe I wasn't ready to let it go. I am now."

"I don't want this back, Reggie. It was for you."

"It belongs in your family, Nigel, not mine."

Nigel shook his head. She knew he was fighting a losing battle over the past. Regina saw the disappointment in his face, but it had to be this way. She went back to the dining table and sat down, turning to look at him seriously.

"Now it really is over between us. There's no reason we need to have contact again."

"Reggie, this isn't what I wanted to happen. I want us to have—"

He moved to touch her, but she pulled away. His touches made her stop thinking straight, and right now, she needed all of her faculties.

"I know this seems crazy after…last night."

"Last night was something special. Don't throw it away."

"I…I'd just been holding so much in for so long. I guess

it all came out. I didn't mean for that to happen. I didn't know it would happen. I shouldn't have let it happen."

"It was meant to happen. It's always been that way between us."

She shook her head and picked up the check from last night, which was still on the table.

"And this." She ripped it up like she had the other one. "I'm doing fine on my own, and there is no…child…that you need to care for."

It was ending, really ending, and her heart had grown heavy with the reality of it, as heavy as the look on Nigel's face.

She took a teddy bear out of one of the bags on the seat next to hers. It had on a baseball jersey and a cap and had a bat sewn to its hands. It brought tears to her eyes, but she didn't let them fall.

"Reggie, we're not meant to end."

"We ended a long time ago. Over six years ago."

She turned the teddy bear around in her hand and found a string to pull to make it talk. She fingered the string but didn't pull it.

"Do you know anyone you can give these to?"

Nigel took a deep breath and looked at the bear in her hands, seeming to feel the same wistfulness she did.

"I have little cousins."

"Good."

She shook her head. There was one more thing that she wanted to say.

"Nigel, I'm sorry…it has to end this way."

But that wasn't what was on her mind. It wasn't what was in her heart. She was thinking about having lost their child, but she had no way to speak her shame.

"It shouldn't end this way. It doesn't have to."

"Yes, it does."

* * *

Nigel carried his packages back down to his car with a heavy heart. He'd almost had it all back, but now he didn't have any of it. He could have spent all day trying to convince her to give them a chance, but until she could forgive him, he knew that no effort on his part would make a difference.

He opened his trunk and put in the packages. There was no need to keep them now. There was no boy, no girl.

He would have taken the day off if she had been willing to spend it with him. Now he had an hour to get to his place, shower, shave, change clothes and get to the office. Fine.

He'd gone from ecstasy to despair in less than twenty-four hours, and now she had simply shut him down. But he wasn't going out like that. He had worked too hard to get this far. He would have to bide his time until he could come up with a new point of entry, a new way to get her to soften her heart to him. It still wasn't over, not yet.

Chapter 4

It had been two weeks since she had seen Nigel, and Regina's spirits were finally picking up after the emotional turmoil. She had her focus back, and she had an on-site installation to keep her busy.

"Are you going to take off from your morning job tomorrow to get the installation done?"

Amelie was at a workstation in the back of the studio stringing an elaborate necklace—one with rows of turquoise and cowrie shells that tapered to a long V. They didn't have any customers at the moment, so she and Regina could chat across the back of the shop.

"No, I'll still need the money," Regina said. "That's the only reason I have that secretary job to begin with—steady income until our income here gets steady. Will you be able to stay late next week so that we don't have to shut down too early?"

"Yeah, no problem. I've already covered all of my evening jewelry-making classes at the bead shop. We'll only have to close early one day."

Regina had a large order to install in a couple of weeks—a custom kitchen backsplash that she'd been working on for most of the last month. It would bring in some much-needed money, so she had to forgo her hours at the store. Half of the money that came in would be going to renovations, so it was worth losing some income at the store.

"I can't thank you enough," Regina said with a smile.

"No prob. You cover for me enough, and you're here more hours than I am anyway."

"Yes, but right now, your beadwork is bringing in more income than the mosaic pieces."

It was true. Amelie was a talented bead artist and sold beadwork supplies as well as her own pieces—mostly jewelry but also hair accents, art objects and even some clothes.

"Oh, mostly the small stuff. My biggest pieces are still sitting here."

"As are mine."

Regina made more from her installations than from the studio, but she did mosaics of just about everything one could think of. She had her standing art pieces, but she also did tables, mirrors, planters, sculptures—anything strong enough to stand a layer of tile and grout. For installations, though, she did kitchens, pools, walks, stairs and fireplaces. She'd even done a patio once.

"You know what we need?" Amelie said. "A showing."

"After we finish the renovations, we should have a real grand opening."

"And we need to change the name."

"Actually," said Regina, "we need to do that now. I've been looking into getting our website back on track, and

we should get all the updates done at the same time—
save money."

"Speaking of which, I got information about the semi-
nars at the community center you mentioned—the ones I
signed us up for."

Regina looked up from the tiles she was laying out.
"Excellent. I've been working on the paperwork, but it's
like figuring out tax forms. Why didn't they teach us this
business stuff in college?"

"At least you went to college."

"Girl, you did, too. You just took your classes in different places one by one. Then you taught yourself. I ad-
mire you for that."

Amelie looked up from her necklace and smiled.
"Thank you, sweetie. About the name, we need to get
something Black in there, let people know that there are
some sisters up in here with some culture."

"I agree with you there. I actually want to do some more
African sculptures. When the front is redone, we can put
them in the window with some of your work that has the
cowrie beads. More than half of what we do has a Black
flavor. We need to find a way to announce that."

"And we need some incense."

"No." Regina groaned and waved her hand in front of
her face. "We have enough smells in here with the paints
and the clay and your soldering and the hot glue."

"That's why we need the incense."

"No, our classes will pass out from all the fumes."

The door chime sounded as a couple came in. Amelie
winked over at Regina; it was Regina's turn to see to the
customers. She pushed her mosaic onto the table, grabbed
a wet rag to get the mastic off her hands and got up to ap-
proach the couple.

"Good afternoon. Can I help you find anything today?"

Regina showed them her various mosaic pieces and then the beadwork. They stopped for a long time in front of one of her favorite mosaics, a large piece of a woman in a sarong looking over a patio at the ocean and horizon. They seemed interested in it and took one of her business cards from the counter. They even looked over her portfolio of in-home installations, but Regina couldn't tell if they would come back.

By the time she was done, Amelie had already begun wrapping up her project and getting ready to leave for the afternoon, as usual.

Mr. Lundstrum came in just before she left.

"Regina has our rent check ready for you, Mr. Lundstrum."

"I do. It's under the register," Regina said.

Their landlord was an old man and walked with a cane. It was clear that he hadn't had the ability to look after this place for a long time. But he was pleased with the upgrades they'd made and liked having them as tenants.

"Come, my dears. I have a bit of hard news."

"What is it?" Regina asked, worried that something had happened to his wife, who was also getting on in years and was not as agile as her husband.

"Well, this won't be easy for you to hear."

He settled down in one of the chairs at Regina's worktable and sighed heavily.

"You know I've been waiting for you to come up with the down payment on this place. You had first refusal."

"Oh, no." Regina could tell what he was getting ready to say, and her heart sank.

"What? What is it?" Amelie hadn't caught the clue.

"You've taken another offer on the house, haven't you?"

"I'm sorry, dear. I just had to."

Amelie turned to Regina. "What are we going to do?"

"Mr. Lundstrum, can't you give us more time? I have an installation in a couple of weeks. That's a couple of thousand dollars. We can give you that. It's not the down payment, but…"

Regina didn't know what else to say. Thankfully, Amelie stepped in.

"We have a good portion of it saved up, and we're looking for a small-business loan now. Just a little more time is all we need."

"I'm so sorry. My granddaughter starts her junior year at American University in a couple of months, and we're strapped. Retirement and the rent on this place haven't been enough, with school bills and all. We needed somebody who could pay now."

The old man took off his glasses and wiped his eyes. His sight was going, as well.

"Gentleman in a fine suit came in willing to pay more than we're asking—pay it now, one time. Wife and I couldn't say no. Was like looking a gift horse in the mouth."

"Oh, no," said Amelie. "What do we do now?"

"Isn't there anything we can do, Mr. Lundstrum? Anything?" Regina asked.

"I'm so sorry, girls. We just had to take it. Wife wouldn't want me to tell y'all, but the savings is almost gone—with the economy and all. This way we can pay tuition and put some in the bank to replace what's gone."

Regina sighed heavily. "I understand."

"We wanted it to go to you, help y'all out. But weren't no way we could wait. Look, I know it's hard. You just forget about the rent this month and the month after that."

"We can't do that," Regina said firmly. "Can we contact him, Mr. Lundstrum—the gentleman who's buying the place? I know it's a long shot, but maybe if he hears us out, if he knows how much we've put into this place already, maybe he'll let us have it after all."

The old man patted his pockets. "I know I've seen his card. Had one of those little cases you hold business cards in. I think I gave it to the real-estate agent we got to handle the sale for us. I'll get it for you, but dear—" he looked at Regina "—don't hold out hope for that. He'll want more than you were going to pay."

"I know you're right," Regina said, "but we have to try."

"I'll bring you the information tomorrow."

"When do we have to be out?" Amelie asked.

"Six weeks from the first of next month. I wanted to give you some time to find someplace new to sell your things."

"Six weeks for upstairs, as well?" Regina asked.

"Yes, ma'am, the whole building's gone. He worked for some kind of investment firm. He'll probably turn it into another restaurant or something. Said he had someone come check it out just a couple of weeks ago."

Regina went to the cash register and returned with the rent check.

"Here is this month's rent. We wouldn't think of not paying it."

Amelie gave her a wry look but went along.

Mr. Lundstrum crumpled the check in his hand and left it on the table.

"No, dear, no. You'll need that to find another place to live in, another shop. I know I'm going back on my word to you. I told you I would wait and sell this place to you, didn't I? Give you time to fix it up a bit and get her going. Didn't I?"

Tears filled Regina's eyes and spilled down her face. Her dream for the shop was being ripped away. "Yes."

Amelie's arms went around her shoulders and the two women hugged one another.

"Don't cry," Amelie said. "You never cry. Now you'll start me crying."

But Amelie was already crying, as well.

"I gave my word," said Mr. Lundstrum. "And here I am going back on it. It's the last thing I wanted to do. And you've got only two months to figure things out and move. I'm so sorry, girls. We just had to take it. Else I don't know what we'd do for tuition next fall. But that means the least I can do is cut you some slack on the last two months of rent. I won't take it, no matter what you do."

"We appreciate it. We really do," Amelie said.

Regina pulled herself together and let out a deep sigh.

"Thank you, Mr. Lundstrum. Thank you. We understand that you would have waited for us if you could have. And we appreciate you giving us a break on the rent to help us move."

"Y'all start looking for a place right away. Won't be easy to find one in this neighborhood."

"It'll be impossible to find one here," Amelie said, but Regina gave her a look that stopped her from going on.

"We'll start looking," Regina said. "I'll let you know what we find."

After walking Mr. Lundstrum to the door, Amelie flipped the store sign to Closed and locked the door and leaned against it.

"What are we going to do?"

Regina heard the devastation in Amelie's voice.

"I don't know. I don't know. This changes our whole business plan—everything. We'll need to find a new space—"

"And it sure won't be in the art district," Amelie said.

"There isn't a vacancy anywhere around here, and if there is, we can't afford it."

"We can check, but I know you're right. That's how we ended up here."

Regina was on the verge of tears again. She looked around the shop, at all they had done already, all the money they'd invested in fixing things up. But she didn't want to give in to those tears. It wasn't hopeless; it was just overwhelming.

"We can't figure it all out right now," she said. "Let's finish the day as usual and then start to create some kind of plan tonight—when to go looking for other places, how to move things, where things can go in the meantime."

"You're right. I have to get these pieces to the consignment store and then get to my sister's shower with a present. It's too early to panic," Amelie said, but Regina could read the disappointment in her voice. "Let's talk tonight."

After Amelie left, Regina tried to carry on with her regular tasks, but her mind kept churning. If they couldn't find a place in the art district, maybe they should try to get a space downtown. But that would be way out of their price range. Their business proposal wouldn't float without a location. They even needed an address for their website.

She worked as efficiently as she could on the mosaic for the installation. All of a sudden, that project took on a whole new significance. A couple thousand dollars could make a big difference right now for her apartment search.

Of course she had some money in her savings, and she had her morning job, which could always pay rent. And her parents would always let her come back home temporarily, but she had no intention of asking them for assistance. She had to figure this out.

A man had come in offering more than the asking price

for the place. He probably knew it was worth more than Mr. Lundstrum was asking, too.

Regina's mind suddenly flew to Nigel—flashing five-thousand-dollar checks around and wearing his fancy suits. He had had a case for his business cards, and if she remembered correctly, his card said he worked at an investing firm. He was also the only one she could think of who hadn't come in shopping. Could he have been the one to make an offer on the place? Did he know that she was planning to buy it? He could see that they were trying to fix it up; he might have assumed that they were trying to get it. If it was him, she was going to be angry as a wet cat.

In fact, the more she thought about the possibility, the angrier she got. Maybe he wanted it as leverage to try to get her back. There he was thinking he could buy her again. Or it could be that he was trying to get back at her for not seeing him. Or… What else, she didn't know, but she sure as hell was going to find out.

It was three o'clock, and no customers were there. She could close the store for a couple of hours and probably not miss a sale. She called Amelie to let her know, ran upstairs for Nigel's business card and got in her car.

Chapter 5

She could tell from the outside of the building that she would feel out of place entering the investment and accounting firm of Hoffman, Johnson and Dowd, and when the elevators opened on their floor, she knew she hadn't been mistaken. They had plush beige carpets, mahogany furniture and expensive art in the lobby, and she was greeted simultaneously by two receptionists. Everything about the place was swank.

"How may I help you?" one of the receptionists asked.

"I'm here to see Nigel Johns, and no, I do not have an appointment."

"Who may I say is here?"

"Regina Gibson."

"Does he know what you're here about?"

"I believe he does."

"He has someone in his office right now, but as soon as he's free, I'll let him know. Please have a seat."

The receptionist gestured toward the waiting area, but Regina didn't feel like sitting down.

"Can I get you coffee, a soda?"

"No, thank you."

She remained standing but moved off to the side.

She spotted the door marked Nigel Johns from her spot in front of the receptionist's desk, and though she didn't have an appointment, she moved right for it when she saw it swing open. Her orange capris, African-print chemise tank and flat gold sandals may not fit in with the decor, but her anger made her more than assertive.

Just inside the door, she found Nigel hugging a tall Black woman who was holding a toddler on her hip. The little boy looked like Nigel, and Regina's temper flared even more. It would make sense that he'd fathered another child or two after leaving her, reckless as he was. And if he already had another child of his own, why would he come worry her about theirs?

He seemed surprised to see her. He must have read the anger in her gaze as jealousy because he immediately introduced his guest.

"Regina, please meet my cousin Michelle and her son, Andre. We were just saying goodbye."

Regina didn't feel like being pleasant, but she nodded at the woman and moved out of the way for them to leave. She shouldn't have let them spike her temper anyway. He had a right to his life, whatever it was. Why should she care?

Nigel stuck his head out of the door behind them to speak to one of the receptionists. "Please tell Mr. Harris that I'm running a bit late. I'll see him shortly."

He closed the door and turned to her.

"My cousin Michelle just moved to DC from down South after a vicious divorce. She needed to get away. I'm helping her out a little, just to get her on her feet. And

Andre is just a doll. I gave him some of the presents that I had for..."

He didn't know how to finish, and she wasn't interested in helping him.

"All the ones that weren't too big for him, he got."

He strolled back to his desk and perched his behind on the front side of it—all businesslike in his tailored black suit and red power tie, all innocent-looking, as if he hadn't pulled the rug out from under her.

"That's none of my business," Regina said, spitting anger.

He seemed a bit confused by her tone.

"It's been over two weeks," he said. "I thought you had written me off for good, but I'm glad to see you. You look beautiful."

She glared at him, waiting for his pleasant exterior to crack and reveal the louse he was, but he just leaned against his desk, waiting. He seemed to fit in here. His Italian watch shone above his French cuff, and his class ring glistened on his finger. She hadn't noticed it before; he must have finished school after all.

"I think you know why I'm here."

"I know why I want you to be here. But no, I don't have any idea why you're actually here. You seem angry. Have I done something? Is something wrong?"

"Nigel, stop playing. You've made a nice little niche for yourself here."

He smiled proudly at her acknowledgement, ignoring the unpleasant tone that accompanied it.

"So why are you trying to take mine away?"

He leaned forward, concerned. "What are you talking about? If anything, I wanted to make things easier for you, not take anything away."

"Well, your little ploy hasn't made it easier. You've

made it harder. Much harder. There's nowhere else in the art district that we could get for that kind of money. What are you going to do with it? Turn it—"

She had started pacing furiously, her cotton capris swishing in the hush of the office. She was trying not to let her voice escalate, but she was distraught, and she was wearying of his innocent act.

"Reggie, sit down."

He tried to put his hand on her shoulders, but she twisted free of his reach.

"Reggie, sit down, and tell me what's wrong."

His voice was low and soothing, but she wasn't about to be lulled by it, not again.

"Did you know we were going to buy it, or did you just decide to snap it up for fun?"

"Reggie, I haven't snapped anything up. Tell me what's going on. Maybe I can help."

"No, I'd say you've done enough. Wouldn't you?"

"Regina, calm down. Sit down. Talk to me. What is it that I've done?"

She stopped pacing and stood her ground to look him right in the eyes.

"Did you or didn't you buy the studio right out from underneath us?"

"Oh, no." Nigel went to her and stopped right in front of her. "I assure you that I didn't, and I didn't know about it either."

He spoke firmly, looking right at her. She scanned his face for a lie, but his features only registered sincerity. If anything, he seemed surprised by her accusation. And worse, he also seemed concerned.

She had no choice but to believe him. She finally sat down in one of the chairs facing his desk. She just sat and stared at the carpet while the anger drained out of her and realization dawned. She should have waited until tomorrow, when Mr. Lundstrum would be bringing her the information on the buyer, rather than rushing over here.

"I do purchase and resell property from time to time. But if I had purchased it, it would have been to give to you, not to take from under you."

"I don't know what I was thinking. Except there you were flashing money in my face, and then…I called things off between us."

"I'm not vindictive, Reggie."

Regina threw her hands up. "*You* I could fight. But now there must be someone else who bought the property, and there's nothing I can do."

There were tears in her eyes, but she wasn't going to let them win. The last thing she wanted was to have Nigel comfort her again. She didn't want to seem like she was overly emotional or like someone who needed a man. She'd been doing okay on her own so far without him. She stood.

"I'm sorry to have bothered you."

"Wait," he said, cornering her in front of the chair until she sat down again. Then he took the other chair. "Let's talk about this. I didn't buy it, but maybe I can help you get it back. As I said, I do invest in real estate sometimes—buy old places, fix them up, make a little money. I have some experience in this kind of thing. I can afford—"

"No, I'm sorry to waste your time."

"Why not let me try to help you?"

"I don't want to owe anything to you or anyone else. My business partner and I will figure it out."

"Why are you being so mule-headed? Maybe I can help. Think of it as repayment for—"

"There's nothing you need to repay me for."

"Then let me try to acquire it, and you can buy it from me."

"No, I'm sure the new owner has plans for it. It's a perfect location. And we weren't ready to make the purchase anyway."

She stood again, feeling small in her flat sandals and out of place next to his black suit, which dominated the posh office space.

"Please, Reggie, don't go. I might be able to help."

"I've bothered you enough. I'm sorry—for everything."

He put his hands on her shoulders to keep her from fleeing. She stared at his chest, feeling as stupid as could be. Then he cupped her chin to raise her face to his.

"It will be okay. I don't know if I can help, but I'd like to try."

She pushed his hands away and straightened. "No, I'll be fine. It was my mistake."

Head held high, she walked through the reception area as fast as her sandals would carry her.

Once outside, Regina stopped for a newspaper and went back to the studio, feeling like a fool for having barged into Nigel's office slinging accusations. To add to her embarrassment, he had been nothing but concerned and kind the whole time. Her reaction seemed so silly now. Anyone walking by could have scouted their studio and seen that it was a perfect location. And in the DC area, there were probably a thousand investors with tailored suits and business-card holders. It just so happened that Nigel Johns was the only one she knew.

And that was the other news of the day: Nigel Johns was now a well-tailored investor-accountant who worked at a top firm and was totally at home in that world. How had he gone from the brother with baggy pants to that?

Regina shifted her mosaic to the side and started looking in the paper for rental spaces where they were—near the Torpedo Factory in Alexandria, Virginia, not that far from downtown DC. There was nothing on King Street, nothing on Union Street, nothing listed for the area at all. She would have to try online later that night.

In the end, she tried to concentrate on the mosaic for the installation, but the news of losing the place still occupied the center of her mind. They were just starting out but had been knocked off their feet, and she didn't know if they could get up again.

She was also trying to pull her face out of the mud after the tantrum she'd thrown in Nigel's office. The tables seemed to have turned. She had gone from being the one telling a bumbling boy to get his act together to being the one whose life was falling apart. And it was falling apart in front of him.

Maybe that shouldn't matter, but it did. It stung like a slap to the face. And worse, she had cracked open a door that she had wanted to keep closed. Now he wanted to help. Hopefully he would remember that she didn't want and didn't need his help.

Chapter 6

Nigel pulled one of his best suits out of the closet and laid it on his bed. It had been almost a week with no sign of Regina since she'd left his office, and he was going to see if she would have a late dinner with him after closing the shop. He hadn't called because she would have said no, but he hoped that if he showed up, he could change her mind.

He needed to see how she was doing, and he wanted to talk to her more about helping her to get the property back for the studio. He had done an online search for the address and had started making calls almost as soon as she left his office, and it didn't take him long to find out who was brokering the purchase, who was buying the location and how much they were paying.

As pigheaded as she'd been at the firm, he expected to have a hard time getting her to let him help, but he was pursuing it anyway. She'd frustrated him to no end in his office, not because she'd accused him of deliberately buying it out from under her but because she wouldn't let him help.

He sprayed some cologne across his chest and pulled on one of his Italian dress shirts. She had come to the office in her casual work clothes, but she had looked amazing. Even when she was ranting at him and pacing his office, he could remember feeling her in his arms, feeling her beneath him.

She'd had on a sleeveless top, which made him want to touch her shoulders, and it was made of two layers of a sheer printed material. It would be cool in the heat, but it made him want to run his fingers over her breasts until he raised the nipples. Even more, he wanted to run his tongue along the curve of the fabric until she moaned the way she'd done that night.

He pulled on his slacks and took a belt off the hook. Even her pants, which came down just below her knees, had made him want to caress the bare curves of her calves and squeeze the rounded globes of her behind. He remembered the way she felt when he had lifted her against him, and it made his knees weak.

He slipped a tie from the rack, looped it under his collar and began tying the knot at his throat. He had been wanting her since she'd given him back his grandmother's ring, but he had stayed away. Seeing her standing in his office had been a gift that made his pulse race.

He hoped to see her tonight again, but this time just to talk, just to get her to stop being obstinate and let him help her. He wanted more, but he would have to wait for that—maybe forever.

Nigel finished dressing with a pair of silver cuff links. At his car, he checked his tie in the window before opening the door, and then he was on his way.

When he got to the studio, he saw that it was still open and parked out front.

Once he got inside, though, he saw that they were already beginning to dismantle the place. Boxes were piled up in the back room and along the back walls. Display cases had been broken down and moved to accommodate the piles of packing paper, bubble wrap and boxes that were lined along the walls and shelves. Only the finished pieces at the front of the studio were still on display.

"Hi, can I help you with anything?"

It wasn't Regina. It was a shorter woman wearing big African-print pants with braids piled high on her head.

"You weren't here when I came last time. I'm looking for Regina Gibson."

"You just missed her. She's on her way home."

"I'll head out back, then."

Nigel stopped, intrigued by the other woman and the possibility of finding out more about what was going on with the studio. He turned back.

"Are you her partner?"

"Yes, hi." She came to shake his hand. "I'm Amelie Richards. Were you looking at a particular piece? Perhaps I can help you."

"No, I'm an old friend of Reggie's. I wanted to help her look into getting this place back. I didn't know that you'd be packing up so soon."

"We tried to get it back, and Regina even talked to the man who's buying it, but it seems like a done deal."

Nigel thought he knew better but left it alone.

"Mr. Lundstrum would have waited for us if he could, but he has his own worries."

He knew that name from the research he'd done so far.

"Do you have a card?"

"Yeah, right by the register."

Nigel wandered toward the register to pick up the card. Amelie had gone back to packing beads into little plastic baggies and throwing them in a large box.

"Do you guys have any plans for what to do next?"

Amelie seemed to become lost in thought for a moment and then shook herself out of it. "We're trying just about everything we know. We're looking for other places. We're checking into consignment shops. We've ruled out anything in the immediate area being in our price range, so we're spreading our net wider. All of that to say 'we don't know.' I wish we did, but right now, it's all up in the air."

Nigel already liked Amelie. At least she would talk to him, confide in him. He had probably learned more in the last five minutes than he would get all evening with Regina.

"Why are you packing up so soon? You don't have to be out yet, do you?"

"We have a few more weeks, but we want to do most of the moving ourselves to save on the cost of movers. It means we need to start now. We'll still need movers for the heavy stuff—the tiles, the kilns."

Nigel leaned against the counter near the register.

"I'm sorry for your loss. I know it meant a lot to both of you."

"You make it sound like a person. But I guess in a way it is like that. It hasn't been easy letting it go." Amelie's eyes misted over, and for a moment, Nigel thought she might cry, but she didn't. She sighed and went back to the beads.

"Where do the boxes go from here?"

"Beadwork comes home with me. Regina has to move as well, so hers are along the back for now."

"Why not rent a storage compartment until you can move into your new place?"

"We thought of that. But we don't know how long it will

be, and we both need to keep working on our art or there won't be income coming in. And Regina has a big installation she's working on this week. I don't know how she's getting it all done."

Nigel had gotten comfortable talking to Amelie. It was nice to ask questions and actually get answers. From what she said, he knew he had to continue pursuing the possibility of getting the property back for them. More than ever, he wanted to be of help to Regina.

"Hey," she called to him, making him stir from his place against the counter. "If you want to catch Regina, you'd better get a move on."

"Okay."

"She left a little early to get ready for a hot date—finally. That one needs a life more than anyone I know."

"A date?" Nigel stiffened.

"Yeah."

"Is it that tall guy?"

"Hah. Not on your life," said Amelie. Then she laughed. He didn't get the joke. "No, this is a real date. You better run along to catch her."

"I'll do that. It was nice to meet you, Ms. Richards."

He had intended to talk to Regina about getting the property back, but now that his temper was piqued by the prospect of Regina going out on a date, he knew he should just go home. He could see her another time, talk to her another time.

Ignoring his better judgment, he headed up the back steps, taking two at a time, and rang her buzzer.

She opened the door with her back to him and one hand coiled around her hair, letting in, presumably, her date.

"I'll be ready in one minute. Sit down for a sec."

Nigel hesitated in the doorway. As she walked away, he could see that she had on a blue dress that flared around her bottom. She also had on heels, showing off her beautiful calves.

Seeing her look so beautiful made his manhood swell. Knowing that she looked so beautiful for another man spiked his temper even more. He should have turned to go right then, but he told himself that he was only there to talk to her about the property. Dinner would be out of the question now, but maybe they could set up another date. A date. The irony wasn't lost on him.

He didn't get the full effect until she came back, and he saw that her hair was wrapped upward and spilling over the top of her head and around the soft curves of her face. The blue dress didn't reveal a great deal, but it seemed to cling to the shape of her body. With her hair pulled up, he could see that she had on a pair of Amelie's beaded earrings, ones that dangled down to her collarbones and accented the shape of her neck. She was beautiful, ready to go out for the evening, and it made Nigel even angrier.

She was surprised to see him.

"I didn't know I let you in."

"You should glance through the peephole before you open the door," he said and came to stand in her dining room. "You look beautiful. Where are we going tonight?"

She seemed excited about a night on the town, and she wasn't even angry at his sudden appearance.

"I'm afraid *we're* not going anywhere. *I'm* going out. So there."

He raised his eyebrows at her unusually good mood, and she chuckled.

"Wait, let me explain. I'm in an odd mood tonight. I've been letting things get me down recently, and I've decided that I'm going to try not to do that any longer. And when do I ever get out for a night on the town? So tonight is a night off from my problems. I won't speak of them. And since I'm not talking about my problems, and you being one of my problems, you should leave."

She pointed him to the door, giving him an impish smile.

He had only intended to talk to her, but the grin on her face inflamed him. He narrowed his eyes and stepped closer to her, wondering if she would be so devilish in his arms. Before he knew he would do it, he had wrapped her in them, had lowered his face to hers and had started to kiss her.

She laughed in his mouth, and her hand came up between them, but it wasn't really a struggle. She must have expected him to let her go, but he didn't, not until her lips had softened and her palm had come to rest upon his chest.

Then he pulled his head up, but she didn't back out of the circle his arms formed around her body.

"I'm sorry, Reggie. I couldn't resist with you smiling that way."

He expected her to get all fiery, like usual, but apparently she was in a playful mood that wasn't dampened by his audacity.

"Stop now. I have someone coming."

She tapped on his chest with her hand, a signal for him to let her go.

"Are you sure you want me to let you go? You look so sexy in your high heels."

"Thank you, but yes."

"I'm not convinced."

He had only intended to talk to her, but now that she was in his arms, he wanted so much more than to talk. He leaned toward her again, taking her hand from his chest and wrapping it around his neck. She let out a startled chirp as his mouth covered hers again—this time for real, this time claiming hers for him and no one else.

He parted her lips with his own and used his tongue to find hers. With her impeding arm now around his neck, he pressed her body close to his until her chest came to rest against his blazer. He stepped even closer, until her thighs were settled against his legs. With his tongue moving deeper into her mouth, he ran his hand up and down her back, pressing her body against his.

Finally, he heard her murmur, and the sound was triumph to his ears.

He came up for air, pressing his forehead to hers and smiling. She must have seen the victory in his eyes because she swatted his arm and laughed.

"There's something between us, Reggie."

"I admit you can have an effect on me." She stepped back. "But I think that's all it is—a lingering effect from the past. Now you have to be going."

He stepped toward her again, bringing his forehead down to touch hers. He had only intended to talk to her, so maybe he should have taken her cue, but he didn't want to let go of her.

"I thought we could talk about getting this place back for you. Come to dinner with me."

"I can't. I have a date. And I've already looked into…" She paused when he placed a soft kiss on her temple. "…all of that."

He was right there, and he loved her. But she still insisted on going out with someone else. Jealousy flared in him again, reviving his temper. If he'd taken her cue, he'd have been on his way to his car by then. Instead, he was on his way to letting his temper get the best of him.

"So how many boyfriends do you have?"

He regretted the words as they flew out of his mouth, and he felt her stiffen in his embrace and begin to push off. He opened his arms to let her go.

"There's the tall guy who came to get his son the first night I was here. And now this is a different one."

He shouldn't have said it, but his anger spurred him on, and it was out before he could check himself. "Are any of them serious?"

"Don't you dare talk to me that way."

The fire was back in her eyes, and her shoulders were pulled back again.

"You don't know anything about my life."

"No, I guess I don't." He couldn't hold back the sarcasm, even as he wondered how things had gotten so far from his original intention.

"You're right about that. Now, it's time for you to go. I have a date."

"Well, I'll leave you to it, then."

"You're good at that. And while you're at it, do me a favor and leave me alone for good."

He knew he shouldn't, but he turned back one more time, unable to resist a final barb.

"So you really want me to leave you alone? Not like the first time when I was supposed to read your mind?"

She had gotten a light silk wrap, and she now flung it over her shoulders angrily.

"Yes. Hell, yes. Leave."

He turned and headed out the door just in time to hear another car pull up out back. Now, as he got to the bottom step, he angrily butted his shoulder against that of the guy on his way up—the date.

He was average-looking, average height, nothing special—nothing to get worked up over. Except that he had a date with Regina.

Nigel banged his car door shut, started the engine and tore a path from the studio. The high and low of the evening had him thinking that loving someone shouldn't feel

like being on a carnival ride all the time. But that was
the problem. He did love this woman, and he was jealous enough to prove it. He had taken her good mood and
turned it into ire. He had just intended to talk to her about
the property, but now they were as antagonistic as ever.
All of this gnawed at his mind while his body still wanted
to hold her.

Chapter 7

She'd had enough.

She caught sight of Nigel's antics on the bottom step and slammed the door. One moment, she was entertaining the idea of a night out on the town. The next moment, he was ruining the highest spirits she'd had since they'd gotten the devastating news about the studio.

She had just wanted a night in which she didn't have to think about all of it. And she hadn't been out with anyone in years. In fact, it was with some hesitation that she had accepted the invitation from the package carrier who made deliveries at the architectural firm where she worked in the mornings. He'd asked her out several times and seemed sweet enough. There weren't sparks, but he seemed nice enough to have a dinner with.

She'd just wanted to get out and not worry about... everything. It felt good to be dressing up and going somewhere, not with friends but with someone new, someone who suggested at least the possibility of a relationship in her life.

Even the sight of Nigel in the doorway hadn't put a damper on her humor. She shouldn't have given in to his kiss, but being dressed up made it feel like a thrill to be held. And he did always have that effect on her. Then he'd had the nerve to ask her how many boyfriends she had. She wanted to give him one swift cuff.

Regina's buzzer rang, and she wasn't sure what to do. She didn't really feel like going out anymore.

Her date seemed sweet enough, but she couldn't imagine explaining to him about this other person who'd bumped shoulders with him on her steps. In fact, she couldn't imagine telling him about her past at all. That meant she probably didn't need to go out with him. And that was probably why she hadn't been going out in general.

She was just starting to think that maybe she could start seeing someone again, but now she just wanted to curl up and sleep.

She opened the door to her date.

"Hey, there's been a bit of a hiccup."

"A hiccup?"

He had on a pair of dark slacks and a white shirt, with a vest that had phrases embroidered on it. It reminded her that she'd only seen Nigel in two- or three-piece business suits since he'd reappeared. It was nice for a change, but not nice enough to alter her decision about the evening.

"Would you mind terribly if we cancel for tonight?"

"You're all dressed. You look wonderful. Is something wrong?"

She didn't want to lie to him, but she didn't feel like getting into the real story either. She hoped something vague would suffice.

"I've just had a real letdown. I can't go out for fun tonight. I'll be heading over to a friend's placc in a few minutes. Perhaps another time."

"Do you want to talk about it?" He seemed genuinely concerned.

"No. I don't. I'm sorry to send you away when we had plans, but please understand."

"I can't say I'm not disappointed."

"I was looking forward to a night out, as well." She walked him back toward the door. "I'm sorry."

"You'll let me know when we can go out again?"

"Yes, I will."

She shut the door. She could have put on a smile and gone out, but she didn't want to pretend tonight. She was still too sore to pretend. The nerve of him.

Regina changed into something more comfortable, got in her car and called Jason on her cell phone. She didn't want to stay in after getting all dressed up, even if she had changed, and she could use a friend right now. He was more than happy to have her come over.

Regina was greeted at the door by Ellison, who carried a tired Kyle on his shoulder.

"Hey, sweets." He bent down and kissed her cheek. "You're just in time to say good-night to this one."

The cranky little one said something groggily.

"I can tell. Good night, honey bunny," Regina said and kissed him on the head. "Here, let me take him. I'll help put him to bed."

"Okay," Ellison said, handing Kyle over to her. "I'll find Jay."

"I'm not lost," Jason said as he entered the room.

He bent down to hug Regina and was about to take Kyle.

"No way. I just got him away from that one. I'll help put him down."

"I'll go get the bed ready."

"Okay, have you eaten?" Jason asked.

"No, but you have. I'm okay."

"Not if you're staying over."

"Am I?"

"I'll get you home in the morning. You owe me a pow-wow," Jason said. They headed toward Kyle's room. "Do you mind eating alone? Once we get this little one down, I need to put that little one down."

Regina laughed. Ellison was almost six feet. Only Jason could call him a little one.

"Okay. But don't leave me alone too long."

"I won't."

With the three of them surrounding him, Kyle fell asleep before the story was halfway through, regardless of the fact that the three adults in the room were having a hilarious time trying to do voices for the different characters.

Ellison went up to change for bed while Jason heated up leftovers for Regina and set her a place in the living room in front of the television.

When he was satisfied that she was comfortable, Jason pointed up the stairs. "Are you sure you don't mind?"

She blew him a kiss and answered, "I'm sure."

"I won't be too long."

"You better not be too short either."

They both chuckled.

Regina felt at home and was able to calm down and let the disappointment of the evening drain out of her as she munched on reheated Chinese food. Being with friends who were so loving and so embracing was like being in a warm bubble bath. It felt relaxing. It felt good. And entertaining little Kyle had made her forget all of her troubles for a while.

She flipped through the channels but wasn't in the mood for television, so she put it on mute and curled up on the couch. It felt like home, but it was good to be away from home, too.

Her eyes were closed when Jason came back out. He had changed into a pair of old sweats.

"Are you asleep already?"

"No, just resting. What about the two little ones? Asleep?"

"Yes, both."

Jason pulled her legs up and placed them on his lap. "Elli had to be up before six this morning. Little thing was plumb tuckered out."

Regina smiled, but she was already dreading the moment when the spotlight would turn on her, which it did.

"And you? You've been owing me info for weeks. Who was he?"

Regina let out a breath. She didn't want to talk about it, but she needed to, and at least she was in a space she could trust.

"He's my ex-fiancé."

"Fiancé? You were engaged?"

"For over four years. I broke it off. I was pregnant and needed someone serious or no one at all. I never told him about the baby, and then I lost it."

"I'm so sorry, Regina." He started to rub her feet. It was soothing. "You've been keeping this under wraps, honey. You could have told me."

"I know. It's just something I don't tell anyone, really."

"What happened? Why did it fall through?"

"I don't know. I guess we were too young. We were sweethearts in high school our senior year. We decided to go to the same college and to get married right after graduation. Even that seemed too long to wait, but our parents liked it."

She was quiet for a moment, remembering the good days, when she was lost in his arms and his touch.

"So what happened?"

"By the time I was done with college, we were just in two different places. I knew I had to be serious if I wanted to survive as an artist. My parents wanted me to take a 'safe' job—become a lawyer or get a job in the government or something."

"Don't they all? When I said I was going into art history, mine had a fit."

"I guess so. By graduation, he was running behind. He had gotten caught up in the party life. He was skipping classes. He would have flunked out if he hadn't been so smart. He was spending more time with his buddies on the couch or at dorm parties than in school. And his parents kept sending him money. They didn't know."

Regina sat up, pulling her legs from his lap to tuck them under her but missing the soothing comfort of his hands.

"Sounds like he did have some growing up to do. But you were young, too."

"Yeah, well, that's when the arguments started. I wanted him to take things more seriously so we could start a life together and have a future. He thought I had turned into a bookworm or something, someone who wanted to make him old before his time, someone who didn't know how to have a good time. After a while, we stopped talking so much."

"That must have hurt."

He leaned over to rub her hair and run his fingers along her face down the lines where tears threatened to fall. But she wasn't going to let herself cry.

"It did. We were supposed to be married in four years, and the four-year mark was coming up. Then I found out that I was pregnant—not planned and not for lack of being safe."

"That's one hell of a wake-up call."

"It was for me, but I didn't tell him. I tried to get him to take things more seriously, but the harder I tried, the more it seemed to only make him want to be a kid even longer. That's when things got bad. He was skipping classes and running the streets with his boys even more. Nothing changed. But me, I knew I had to grow up or end up in my parents' house again, and I wasn't going to let that happen. When I realized I'd turned into a nag and when the arguing got bad enough, I called off the wedding and told him to leave. If he wasn't going to grow up, I didn't need him."

She shook her head to wake up from remembering the past and took one of the pillow cushions onto her lap, hugging it.

"How were you going to do it on your own?"

"I don't know, but I was going to try. I was already out to show my parents I could make a life as an artist. I figured I'd just have to show him, too. I planned to raise the baby on my own, and if he ever grew up, so be it. But I wasn't waiting to find out."

"That explains a lot about you. There's an edge to you. Always working hard. Always keeping a bit to yourself. Always determined to figure things out on your own, alone."

"Well, some of it I didn't have to. I lost the baby before I really told anyone and before I really started to show. My parents didn't even know. I thought I would tell everyone after the wedding or at the wedding or something like that."

Jason scooped his arms around her and pulled her between his legs and against his chest, resting his chin on top of her head. It wasn't a sexual gesture. It was a gesture between old friends when one needed solace, when one needed a shielded space from which to speak and in which to be heard. Regina put her arms over the ones that were wrapped around her waist.

"I was alone when it happened. I ended up calling an ambulance, and they took me to the hospital, but nothing could be done. They never knew what went wrong."

"Oh, honey, I'm so sorry."

Maybe it was because she had cried with Nigel, but she didn't cry now. She felt sad, but she could say it without the tears. It still hurt, but the hurt didn't consume her the way it had before, when she had first confessed.

"What about now? What does he want now? Why were you arguing?"

Regina sighed. In order to answer that question, she would have to figure a lot of things out.

"He wanted to take care of his children. He thought Kyle and Tenisha were ours."

"But you never told him. How did he know?"

"Apparently, my college roommate told her boyfriend. Nigel found out from him a few months ago that I was pregnant when I graduated. It's been over six years. How does he expect to waltz back up in here? But here he is, trying to be with me again."

Regina's anger made her restless, and she sat up and turned to face Jason. This might have been a mistake because he peered at her quietly until her anger settled, then he asked her a question.

"And you? How do you feel about him now?"

It was startling because it was a real question, one she was unprepared to answer.

"I don't know. He makes me so angry that I want to be over him. But I don't know."

"Has anything *happened* between you two recently?"

Regina rolled her head to ease her neck; she hadn't realized that she was so tense.

"Ugh. Do we have to go there?"

Jason's wry look said that she couldn't hide from him.

"I already know the answer. Look, it's been a long time since you've been with anyone. Right?"

"Yes."

"It could be him, or it could be that you're just lonely. Find out before you get caught up in something from the past that's not meant to be."

"I think I already know. I think it needs to be over. I just need to convince him of that."

"If it's really over, you'll convince him," Jason said.

"I think I have, and if not, I'm sure I will."

She'd had enough.

Regina woke up the next day before the house had stirred. It was eight in the morning on a Saturday, and her cell phone was ringing in her purse. That could only be one person.

"Hey, Mom."

She uncurled herself on Jason's couch. It was a pull-out, but she didn't need the room and was comfortable on the thick, velvety cushions. She and Jason had stayed up talking, and he had gotten her a pillow and sheets before heading up to Ellison. They were going to have brunch together at ten near the studio so that she could change and open up by noon.

"Hello, sweetheart. I hope you're not still down about that little shop of yours. It'll work out, honey. You'll see. Do you need any money, baby?"

"No, Mom, I'm fine. How are you doing?"

"My knees get to bothering me, but other than that, we're both just fine. Look, I'm calling because your father and I talked it over, and we're coming down to help you move your things into your new place."

Her parents had moved from South Carolina to New Jersey her second year in college.

"Mom, you just said that your knees were bothering you."

"I know, I won't be able to move the heavy things, but I can do some of the packing up while your father helps you."

"I actually have a few friends who are willing to help. I'll be okay."

Regina hated it when her parents treated her like an adolescent, but she also understood that this was their way of feeling involved.

"No, we've done made up our minds. Now, when are you planning on moving so we can figure out when to come down?"

To keep them happy, she would graciously accept their help with a few of the smaller things—not the heavy tile, finished boards, kilns or supplies. The movers would take care of the rest, and she and her parents would be able to spend most of their time enjoying one another. But she had to time it just right to make sure the heavy stuff was out of the way.

"Let me call you back when I get home. I'm over at Jason's now."

"So early?"

"I came by last night, and it got late, so I stayed over."

"That's good, sweetheart. I hate it when you're out late at night. How is little Kyle?"

"He's as adorable as ever. You'll see him when you get here."

"Here, say hello to your father."

"Hi, Dad. Mom's roped you into coming down."

Her father laughed. "Yep, she got her mind set on it. We're just gonna help you move some things. Won't be no trouble."

"It's no trouble having you visit, Dad."

"Good. We'll be seeing you soon. Goodbye, sweet pea."

"Bye, Daddy."

Regina stood and stretched her legs. The house was still quiet; it was two hours before brunch.

Talking with Jason had made her a little raw, and she wondered now about his question. What about her? How did she feel?

She did want it to be over, and she was still angry as all get-out. But she had given in to Nigel, had even let herself be in a playful mood around him. Was she still just getting over him? If so, she needed to do so quickly. She not only had to get on with her life, she had to put it back together again.

Chapter 8

"You okay back there, Andre?"

"Yup." His little cousin was engrossed in the video game that Nigel had gotten him for the ride and didn't look up. He'd been at it for almost an hour.

"Those games were genius." His cousin Michelle winked at him.

"I'm surprised he hasn't fallen asleep."

"If we were at home, he would have napped, but this is too exciting for him."

Nigel pressed the clutch, changed gears and stepped up the speed a notch as they cruised south on I-95. The car trip home was a chance to open up his two-month-old Lexus and see what she could do.

His cousin Michelle needed to get some of her things from home, and he hadn't seen his folks in a while. Rather than having her try to ship things, they had opted for a short trip home. They could pack up his trunk and most of the backseat to bring some of her things back up to DC.

"How much longer until we stop?"

They'd been on the road for four hours. It was an eight-and-half-hour drive to Charleston, but they had decided to make a real trip of it and spend the night in Raleigh.

"About forty-five minutes, maybe less given the time we've made."

"That gets us in at three."

"Here, I got the movie listings online. Find us an animated film we can take Andre to."

"Really?" Michelle seemed surprised.

"Yeah, why not?"

"I thought you might want some time to yourself by then. I didn't know you'd want go to a kids' movie with us."

"Yeah, it'll be fun."

Nigel had noticed that Michelle was always surprised by little things like that. Why wouldn't someone want to go with them to a children's movie? It made him wonder how bad her ex-husband had been and in what ways.

They'd talked for the first hour, and he'd gotten to know her a little better. After that, conversation popped up from time to time, but mainly they turned up the radio and just cruised.

Unfortunately, this part of the trek also made him think about Regina—how much he wished it was her that was riding with him to see his folks, how badly he'd messed up with her. His jealous tantrum had been childish. From her point of view, he'd probably regressed to the way he was before, when they were together in college. No wonder she didn't want him now. Who could blame her?

He had been a child then. And she had grown up. He'd loved her, but she wanted them to act like an old retired couple, and he was all for just having fun. He'd never cheated on her, but while she studied, he got too caught up with the party life at school, mooching off his parents and letting an education pass him by.

They'd been in her apartment when she'd confronted him for the last time. It started as an argument he'd gotten used to. Why wasn't he studying? When was he going to get serious? Then it turned into something else. If he wasn't going to grow up, then he needed to leave. The wedding was off. She was crying. He was hurt and stunned.

"I don't need you," she had said, "so get out—for good." And he had. Now he could see only too well what had driven her to that. He could also see what he had lost, what he wanted back.

If she had been with him in the car now, he could've pulled her over to his side of the seat, nestled her under his arm and rubbed her thigh while they enjoyed the ride.

They pulled into the Raleigh Marriot City Center just as they'd timed it and checked in.

"You guys freshen up, and meet me at my room whenever you're done," Nigel said.

"We won't be long. We just need a potty break. Sorry, I'm used to being around a little one."

"No need to apologize. Take your time."

Nigel took off his blazer, stretched from the hours of driving and lay back on his bed to wait for his cousins. If Regina was with him, they could have spent the whole afternoon making love in the hotel room—right on the bed he was lying on. They could have gone out to dinner when the sun went down and then taken a walk around downtown before it got late.

Back then, he had known they were arguing, but he didn't realize how bad it was or how much they were drifting apart until she'd called off the wedding and put him out. He didn't actually live with her, but he spent more time with her and her housemates at their apartment than he spent in his dorm room, so it felt like being put out. It broke his heart. Whatever was wrong, he had still assumed that they'd always be together.

He heard a knock at the door. "It's just us," Michelle said.

"Ready to head out?" he asked. "Did you pick a movie?"

"I think he'd like *Where's Wellington?* It's a new animated feature from Cypress. You don't have to go unless you really want to."

"I really want to. Is that okay with you, Andre?"

Andre nodded eagerly. Both of the adults chuckled. Nigel picked him up, anchored him on his hip and headed them down the hall to the elevator.

Where's Wellington? turned out to be the most fun he'd had in a long time. The movie was made to be amusing for adults as well as children, but Nigel was equally intrigued by interacting with Andre, who spent much of the movie on his lap, except when he got restless and climbed over to his mother.

Nigel made sure he could reach the popcorn, held the soda for him when he said he was thirsty and tried to keep him relatively quiet. It made him understand what it meant to be an adult responsible for the well-being of a child. It made him miss the child he never had. After the movie, he gave Michelle some money, pressing her to take it, and they went shopping at the stores around the Convention Center to get gifts for the family they were about to see. They had heavy shopping bags, so they headed back to the hotel and had dinner there.

By then, Andre was getting cranky.

"I better go put him down. What time do we meet in the morning?"

"I want to go to the fitness center and the pool before

we go. Why don't we meet at ten-thirty for breakfast and head out at eleven again?"

"Works for me. You heading up now?" Michelle asked.

He didn't want to admit that he would feel alone in his room—alone without a specific person.

"No, I think I'll have some coffee before I head up. I have some work to do tonight, and it'll keep me up for a while."

"Take care, then, cousin. And thank you for…the shopping."

"We're family. You don't have to thank me."

"Yes, I do." She gave him a hug.

While Michelle headed up to her room, Nigel went to the hotel bar. He didn't really want coffee, but it couldn't hurt, and he did have work to do that night. He took a seat at the long, curved counter and ordered his coffee.

It wasn't long before a woman came and sat next to him. She had on a revealing dress and high heels, and she leaned toward him, looking his way from one seat over. She had smooth, ebony skin and her neatly piled dreads were drawn up to the crown of head. She was actually a good-looking woman.

She slid over to the seat next to him. "I'm here for a wedding. Do you mind the company?" she asked.

"Help yourself. No bachelorette party to go to?"

"No. That's over. No naked men."

Nigel looked at her when she said it and found her staring at him. She had wanted to get a reaction out of him, to tell him something unexpected. He thought about a night of hot sex with a random stranger, no strings attached. He couldn't say he wasn't tempted.

"I'm sorry to hear that."

She turned toward him on her stool, letting her foot

come to rest on the back of his calf and looking directly into his eyes.

"I was sorry, too."

Her offer was direct and unmistakable. It was nice being the one who was getting chased for a change. Nevertheless, Nigel had a decision to make.

"Do you have any plans for the evening?" she asked and let her hand drop to his thigh.

He had a decision to make very soon.

Back in his room, Nigel pulled out his laptop and tried to get some work done, but his mind was wandering.

"Unfortunately, I have work to do," he'd said and taken his leave, paying for his coffee and her drink.

He had turned down an offer from an attractive woman, and why? Part of it was because he wasn't actually a player; in fact, it had been a very long time—high school—since he'd been that kind of player.

Mainly, though, he was invested in a woman who wanted nothing to do with him.

"How's that working for you?" he asked himself out loud.

But at the same time, Regina was the reason he had actually been tempted to have a tryst. He wanted to be wanted, needed—even by some random woman. He wanted Regina to know that he was desirable again—to someone.

It wasn't until she had actually put him out in college that he had realized how little she had come to think of him. And that had made him think little of himself. It had made him take a good look at where he was and what he was doing, and he hadn't liked what he saw.

After a couple of months of wallowing, though, he started to tally up the figures, calculate what had caused him to lose her respect, her love. That's when he figured out he was a year behind in school and would be even more behind if he flunked that semester. That's when he woke up.

He wouldn't settle for a partial transformation. He cut off his so-called friends, threw out his CDs, discarded most of his wardrobe, left behind his urban vernacular. He found his schoolbooks, saw his professors, started trying to salvage what was left of the semester. He needed to prove to her that he could make it, really make it. He started plotting for success and all its trappings.

Now, he had those things, and he desperately wanted to go forward with Regina. That's why it had been so stupid to get jealous and act so childishly with her the other night. He'd seen himself devolve into what he was before—an immature kid. When he'd put that person behind him, he'd thought it was for good. He desperately wanted to go forward with her. But he had no inroad now, no reason to call her. Or none that she would listen to. Whatever plan he thought he had was not working, and it had turned into one big up-and-down circus ride.

He was thinking himself in circles and decided to stop.

It was almost one o'clock, and he wanted to make it an early morning. He got undressed and got in bed—alone. He would be able to figure out the next step after a good night's sleep.

It took them less than four hours to make it the rest of the way to Charleston. Nigel dropped Michelle off at her mother's house before three, said hello to his aunt, who gushed over him because of the help he'd been to Michelle, and headed home.

His mother greeted him at the door with a big hug, pulling his head down to take his face in both of her palms.

"My baby. Oh, it's so good to have you home. Come see our son in his new suit," she called to his father.

He towered over his mother, who was barely five-three, so it was always odd to him when she called him her baby, but he loved it nonetheless. It let him know that though he had been away, he was home.

"It's not a new suit, Mom."

"It looks brand-new. Come say hello to your aunt Elizabeth and your cousins and some folks from the church."

Oh, lord. This meant that she'd invited people over to see him. In his "new" suit, no less.

"Where's the new suit?" his father asked, coming out of the kitchen.

"Hey, Pop. It's not a new suit."

His father gave him a brief hug, as was his way, and pulled him into the dining room, where people were eating and talking. Like his mother, his father was showing him off to the family and friends. He made sure he had a polite smile on his face and greeted everyone in turn. Secretly, he also wished that Regina was there so that she would be able to see that he wasn't the same mess-up he used to be.

"We were worried about you there for a while," one of his parents' church friends was saying.

"He just had to find his way," said another. "Each in his own time."

"Hey, cuz, you hungry? Come get a plate."

His cousin Jeremy was just a bit older than he was and could probably see how awkward Nigel felt with people fussing over him. Nigel was glad to have an out and slipped into the kitchen.

"Hey, Jeremy. Thanks."

"Don't mind them. They just want you—and everybody else they know—to know that you done good. You made it."

"I know. I know."

But the person he most wanted to know that he'd made it wasn't there. "You've done well for yourself, too."

"Thanks," Jeremy said. "But I was caught up in stuff, as well. I remember you went through it. It makes them even more grateful when you turn out okay."

The two men chuckled.

"If we'd known," Nigel said, "we could have planned it that way."

"Just remember," his cousin said, "it's about balance."

After he ate, he sat around with his folks and their friends until late into the evening, and after their guests left, he broke out the presents he'd gotten for his parents. His mother got a gold necklace with a heart on it, and his father got a watch for himself and a check for the both of them.

After helping his mother load the dishwasher and watching some baseball with his dad, he finally headed upstairs to change and get to bed. Going into his room had become something of a shock. His mother hadn't changed it since he left for college. It still had his sports trophies on the dresser, his old music posters on the walls, his football-themed bedspread on the bed.

He hung his suits in a closet that still held his high school football jersey and dropped his suitcase on a chest that still held some of his barely used books from his first four years in college.

He fingered the cover of his text for College Algebra, wondering how he had passed the course. Now numbers were a major part of his life. His transformation had taken him longer than he'd thought, longer than he'd wanted. He'd finished college in a year, but the rest—the professional degree, the bank account, the car, the move back to DC—all that had taken him the better part of the past five years.

Maybe if he hadn't waited so long things would be easier now. When his net worth tripled in the past twenty-four months, he had begun to put out feelers for relocation. Then he found out that Regina had been pregnant. It was the news that there was a child that propelled him into real action. The truth was that he didn't feel he'd made it yet—that he was worthy. He was waiting for that, but perhaps only having Regina would make him feel that way: unbroken.

Nigel sat down on his old twin bed and scanned the furnishings of his past.

He had become something very different than this room. He had become grown.

The next day Nigel took his parents, grandmother and aunt out to dinner and would have been content after that to stay home and catch up on some work. Instead, he was heading downtown to meet Jeremy and two of his other cousins and some of their friends at a club.

"They just want to be nice," his mother had said. "It can't hurt to go out for a little while so they know you're family."

He rolled his eyes as he pulled into the lot at the Cheshire Cat. Jeremy clapped his back when he got out of the car.

"Okay, brother, you need to loosen up—a lot. You ready?"

In the day, he'd have liked nothing more than partying with the boys, but now, to be honest, he just didn't know how to anymore. He didn't go to "occasions" unless business called for it, and now he found himself sitting at a table and watching drinks.

"Hey," Jeremy said over the music, "you're out of practice."

"Not in the mood."

If Regina was there, he would have had a reason to dance. It might all come back to him. As it was, he had little to celebrate.

"Aw, what did I expect?" Jeremy teased. "You turned into a nerdy bookworm right before our eyes."

"I think you might be right," his other cousin returned. "Man, you don't know how to get a life anymore. Come, let us school you."

Jeremy got him up and backed him into a woman, giving him a nod and wink. Since it looked like he'd interrupted her, Nigel had no real choice but to ask her to dance.

After two songs, he waved to her and headed back to the table. One of their group had disappeared, and Nigel asked where he'd gone.

"His girlfriend is here. We won't see him for the rest of the night," Jeremy said.

Lucky man.

Nigel got home late that night. He'd enjoyed the music, but he wouldn't be going to clubs with his cousins and friends again on this trip. What the night confirmed for him was that he really was through with the club scene, at least without Regina, and that he wanted her back very much.

His parents were already sleeping when he got home, because church was the next day. He only had until Tuesday afternoon to spend with them before picking up his cousin, packing her things in his car and making the eight-and-a-half-hour trek back to DC. Come to think of it, he should stop tomorrow and get some more games for Andre. This would be a very long trip for him.

He got in bed thinking about Regina. Her parents had lived nearby before they'd moved up to the northeast. She'd been in this house, this room; he'd kissed her on this bed. Now the twin box spring seemed small for him, but he'd love to have her there to try to fit them both in. She'd have to be wrapped in his arms for it to work.

She wanted to be left alone, but as long as there was a chance, he couldn't leave it alone. When he'd moved back up to the DC area to be near her—near them, he had thought—he'd outfitted everything so that she would see that he'd actually made it. Only now she wasn't trying to see his life.

Now they were cut off with no real reason for contacting each other, but he wanted contact.

He needed a new plan.

Chapter 9

Regina kicked off her flip-flops and slipped her feet into black pumps. She tossed the shoes into the backseat, straightened her skirt, grabbed her purse and pulled out her briefcase, the one on wheels. After she pulled up the handle, she checked her hair in the rearview mirror and was on her way.

She was going to the workshops on starting a small business that she'd found at the community center. In fact, a member of National Bank was supposed to be speaking and staying for consultations, so she and Amelie had decided to look the part. If they were close enough to being ready, they could make a contact.

She stopped at the registration desk to sign in and get an information packet. When she'd gotten a Danish and coffee from the breakfast table and had finished pinning on the name tag that they'd given her, she headed down the long hall to the banquet room. She found Amelie inside already, and the two hugged. She looked around nervously. It was a large space set up with rows of tables and chairs. And it was full. In a real way, this was their competition.

Amelie had on a blue linen pantsuit with a white shirt, and her braids were pulled back into a ponytail. She took a second look at Regina.

"Lord, girl, you look like a lawyer. You clean up well."

"I hope it works. Here—" she pulled Amelie down to their seats and opened her case "—let me show you what I've done so far."

She pulled out books and notes and several folders of paperwork. Then she began walking through the paperwork she'd brought, starting at the top.

"That's the proposal you emailed me," Amelie said. "I've read that."

"Yes. That's the three-page version, and this is the thirty-five-page version with your corrections. Here's the thing I couldn't scan. It's a new draft of the loan application. I've put sticky notes with my questions and problems on everything. The two main problems are a space and the financial statement. Oh, and there's collateral. With the old place, we were getting it at such a good price that it became a huge chunk of the collateral. Now, what do we use? All of the estimates we have are for the old space. That would work for a new space too, right? Or not."

Regina pulled out one of the books she'd been using. Then she stopped and put it back. "It doesn't make sense to look at that now."

"And we went over all of this on Saturday. Calm down. At worst, we're just here to get the 4-1-1."

Regina took a breath. "I know. I just feel like so much is riding on this." And it was. If they could get a small-business loan, they could start again. If not... But she felt prepared enough to face people and try to get answers to her questions. It was the first time things felt like they might actually work out since she'd had to move. All they needed was a new space and the loan. Right now, though, Amelie was right—she needed to calm down.

She took the pad of paper and pen out of the information folder, and readied herself for the first session.

"This is a totally professional setup," said Amelie as they looked around.

"I know. And it's free. All the speakers are working professionals in the business, and they're all doing it pro bono."

Amelie turned to her. "You've done an amazing job putting this application together."

"You've been helping, too."

"I know, but you've been leading the charge. I wouldn't have even attempted it on my own. You're the one who's put in the long hours on this. Relax. It'll work out for us. And thank you."

She looked at Amelie's face, and the sincerity there brought tears to her eyes. It had been a lot of work. If they could start again, though, it would be worth it.

"No problem."

She smiled at her friend.

The presenters started pulling down the screen on the platform at the front of the room, setting up AV for the morning sessions. That drew her eyes toward the front table.

And there stood Nigel. He was watching as the screen came down and talking to two of the other people at the head table. A young woman came up to him and handed him some papers. He gave her direction of some kind, and then went back to chatting. After a moment he stopped and went to the AV cart and started doing something with the laptop that was on it.

Regina couldn't believe her eyes. She pulled out the final seminar program from the information packet—the version with all the names of speakers and moderators. There it was. Nigel Johns. He was the moderator for the morning sessions and a speaker on both the morning and the afternoon panels. She flipped to the back. The investment and accounting firm of Hoffman, Johnson and Dowd was one of the contributors.

What was she going to do? He'd insulted her the last time she saw him, and she didn't feel like sitting under his watchful gaze as the absorbent pupil. She'd since decided that she was done with him for good. She didn't want to put herself through this.

She replaced the notepad, pen and program, closed the folder and stood to begin packing up the things she'd pulled out—everything but the paperwork. Amelie would need that.

"What are you doing?"

"I can't stay."

"Why? What's going on? Regina?"

"I'll explain later. I just can't stay."

She glanced up and found Nigel's eyes on her. She pressed her lips together, gritted her teeth and moved more hastily, turning from the table to get the hell out of there.

Amelie grabbed her arm. "You can't leave. We start in less than fifteen minutes."

"I'm not staying." She sat for a moment. "Look—everything is in the folders, and it's all labeled."

"Yes, but you're the one who knows what everything is. You know what questions to ask. I need you here."

"All you have to do is take good notes on what they say. I can't stay for this. I can't be here with him."

"Who?" She followed Regina's glance to Nigel. "Oh. That's the guy who came to see you the night you went out with what's-his-name. Did something happen between you two?"

There was a hint of innuendo in her voice, but Regina didn't have time to correct her or explain.

"Look, I can tell you about it later. For now, I need you to handle it. Just show them what we have so far, and write down whatever they say. I'll leave all the folders. You don't need the books. Can you get the folders in your bag? No, just hold on to the case. We can talk tonight."

She grabbed her purse and hurried out.

Nigel spotted Regina when he turned on the laptop to set up his slide-show presentation. He'd never really seen her in business attire. She was…breathtaking. She was always beautiful, but something about seeing her dressed in the fashion of his world made his manhood stir and begin to menace him something awful. He had to calm his body down.

She had on a navy blue skirt suit that hugged her body the way he wanted to. It was a traditional cut, except that the top tapered toward the waist right where his hands would go, and from there a ruffled hem flared out over her curves. A triangle of her camisole was visible under the jacket above the bust, just below a row of white pearls. Her hair spilled out over her head in neat curls parted on the side, and dangling pearls fell from her ears. He had to control himself or lose his composure, but he'd never wanted to touch and ravish a woman so badly.

He couldn't take his eyes off her, not even when she glanced in his direction and caught him staring. He didn't move until he realized that she was passing her things over to her business partner, as if she was about to leave. When she turned on her heels and hurried toward the back door, he called one of the office assistants to come check the slide show, and sprinted after her.

He stopped at Amelie's table.

"Hello, Ms. Richardson. Where's Regina going? Is she all right?"

"It's Richards—Amelie."

"Sorry. I almost had it."

"That's okay, and so is she. What's going on between you two?"

"I was an idiot is what. Let me go try to catch her. Can I speak with you later, about business? Can I reach you at the number on your card?"

"Yes, you can."

"Good, let me go try to catch her."

She made it out of the large banquet room and halfway down the hall before she heard an out-of-breath voice behind her, getting nearer.

"Wait. Reggie. Don't leave the seminar on account of me. We have good information. I can help you."

"Leave me alone," she said over her shoulder.

He caught her arm at the glass doors leading outside the building, but she didn't stop and pulled away.

"You don't have to leave, Reggie. It's good information."

"I know." She didn't break her stride. "And I have a good partner who can get it for us."

He followed her down the walkway outside, toward the parking lot, his tie flying over his shoulder as he jostled to keep up with her, get ahead of her, stop her.

"Regina, please don't go. I was an idiot when I came by your place. I was jealous and acting like a kid. Don't let it cheat you out of a good opportunity. Don't let my stupidity do that."

She was at her car and found her keys.

"I wouldn't. I'll get what I need to know."

She got in, closed the door and gunned the engine.

He slapped the back hood in frustration as she tore away.

When she got to the end of the row of cars, she slowed down, then stopped. She watched him in her rearview mirror as he headed back up the walk and into the building.

She had stopped at the end of the lot, and she hadn't started again. She just sat in her car with the blinker flashing, torn.

She shouldn't let his foolishness cheat her out of good information. But wasn't she doing just that? At least he had acknowledged that it was foolishness.

"I was jealous and acting like a kid."

Amelie could get the information, but Amelie was also right. Regina had done more of the background work and knew better what questions to ask.

"Don't let it cheat you out of a good opportunity. Don't let my stupidity do that."

She sighed. She needed to get a grip.

A car beeped for her to move and she had to decide. She switched her blinker, turned back into the lot and found another space. She would feel silly going back past the registration desk, but she'd get over it.

She found Nigel bending over her table talking to Amelie.

"You guys have done a lot already. You can walk through it with a lender this afternoon."

When he saw her, he straightened and stepped back for her to take her seat again.

"I'm so glad you came back, Regina."

She nodded noncommittally, and he headed toward the front. It was time to start.

"I'm glad you're here, too, girl," Amelie said. "I didn't know if I could make my way through all of this stuff."

Nigel took the podium to welcome the participants, thank the sponsors, go over the lineup for the day and introduce the first speaker. Seeing him in a business capacity was like seeing a new light. He was all about business, but he was also congenial, humorous, interesting. This was his world, and he was clearly a polished and professional master of it. He went over some statistics on new businesses to end his opening remarks: a third broke even; a third suffered a loss; more than half failed within ten years.

"We're here to arm you with information so that you can supersede those odds."

The morning session on business proposals didn't have as much new information as Regina expected. But it gave her a lot of ways to tweak what they already had to make it better. It also confirmed for her what she had known. They needed to get more information on competition, and they needed to fix their financial section.

It was Nigel who spoke about the financial statements and projections. He seemed at ease in this world, knowledgeable about how it worked. He opened his jacket and stuck one hand in his pocket as he flipped through a slide-show presentation of his major points.

It was all a lot to take in, but it was just as much to take in the professional bearing and acumen of Nigel Johns. At moments he seemed to be staring directly at her as she took notes and absorbed the points he was making. Other times, he panned the room or pointed to the graphs on the screen. He knew statistics off the top of his head. He held everyone's attention. During the question-and-answer session, he received the most queries and was comfortable interacting with the large audience.

"Actually, the financial portion of the business plan

is one of the reasons people hire or consult accountants, like me. Avail yourself of me while it's free." The audience laughed. "And don't be afraid to seek help with this."

He wasn't at all the boy she had known in college. He was sharp and handsome, professional and at ease.

During lunch he was busy making good on his word; people lined up at the speakers' table to ask him questions or have him go over their financial statements. When the line melted away, he brought his box lunch over to their table and turned around one of the seats in front of them.

"Can I sit down?"

"Sure," Amelie offered.

"If I don't eat somewhere else, I may not get to eat at all."

"We understand," said Amelie. "Help yourself."

Regina glared at her for a second, but the gesture went unnoticed.

"Can I check out your financial statements and projections while I'm here? If you don't mind me eating as I do it."

"That—"

This time Regina cut Amelie off. "That section of our plan needs a lot of work. We're not ready to have someone look at it yet."

Amelie's eyes widened, but she said nothing.

"I'm used to seeing partial drafts and that kind of thing. I don't mind taking a look—no judgment."

"If you insist," Amelie said. With some effort, she slipped the folder from under Regina's hands and handed it over to Nigel.

"So how have you ladies enjoyed the seminar so far?" he asked while reading the pages and flipping to the appendices.

Amelie was the first to respond. "It's great. We might

actually be able to get this done. But it's a whole lot to follow, as laypeople."

"I know. I'm for teaching business to everyone in high school and college. It impacts us all. People get to this stage, and it's like taking a crash college course with no intro to soften it."

He took a bite of his sandwich and finished perusing their pages.

"You guys," he said, but he was looking at Regina, "I can tell that you've done your research. This is great. There are some sections that aren't fully done, and it would be better if your business had been making more, but there are ways to pump it up, regardless."

"What's not finished?" Amelie asked.

"Several things. For one, the cash flow projections are presented monthly for the first year and quarterly after that. It's one of the most important parts of the proposal. You also—"

"We know," Regina said. It nettled her to have him critiquing her work. She didn't know why, but she wanted to stop it nonetheless.

"I know you do. I was only explaining to Ms. Richards." His reaction suggested that he could tell that he'd upset her, but he wasn't sure why. Regina had to admit that he wasn't being condescending or unkind. "Look, you've done a huge part of the work. Why not let me help you guys with some of this?"

"That would be great. Do you do private consultations?"

"All the time. And Regina, I would do anything for you. Please know that."

Amelie's eyebrows went up, but Regina remained aloof.

"Think about it, please." He was looking at Regina. "Let's talk more during the breakout sessions this afternoon. Is that okay?"

"You got it," Amelie said.

The afternoon sessions were starting, and even though Nigel wasn't moderating anymore, he was on the panel again, so he had to leave.

"He seems to want to help," Amelie said. "What's up?"

"It's a long story."

"Give it to me, girl."

"We don't have time. This is the session we need most."

Amelie looked at her with skepticism.

"Look," Regina said, "without an address, we don't even know if what we have is useful or if we need to go to a startup loan. In short, we don't know what we're doing anymore."

Amelie finally turned her attention to the moderator, and Regina followed suit.

The afternoon session was more intense than the morning's had been.

Regina listened carefully and took notes. Like the first session, it only confirmed for her how far they had to go. Her determination wasn't wavering, but her confidence was. If they hadn't lost the site, they might be okay, but now...she didn't know.

After the afternoon sessions, the speakers were placed at tables around the room so that people could go to them with questions.

They got a few minutes with the representative of National Bank, who suggested, in short, that they had to find another location before they could finalize the application. After that, they wandered to the other tables with their less pressing questions, and Regina was glad that she'd stayed, because she did know better what to ask. Amelie even pulled her to Nigel's table, where he looked over the drafts of their financial sections and made suggestions.

Nigel had been at his table for the duration of the breakout session but came over to them as the participants were beginning to leave. Amelie and Regina were packing up things at their table, and after a day of taking notes on things that needed to be done, fixed or changed, Regina's spirits weren't very high.

"I'm glad you stayed, Regina."

She nodded her head, not in the mood for chipper conversation.

"Thank you for all your help," Amelie said.

"No problem. Hey, would you guys like to grab dinner and talk more about the business plan and the application needs? We can even set up some consultations. I can help you get the financial sections in order and help you find people to look over the other sections."

Regina could tell that Amelie saw what a resource he could be and was grateful for his offer. "That would be great, and I'm hungry."

"I need to head home," Regina replied. "And if what the lender said is right, the application isn't going anywhere until we have another location."

Nigel didn't back down. "That doesn't mean we can't put the application in order, and Regina, I can help you with the location. I've been looking into the studio site ever since you came to see me, and—"

"Nigel, you've been more than helpful. Thank you." She was clearly shutting him down.

Amelie glared at her but didn't say anything.

"Then why don't we set up a consultation?"

"Yes, Regina, let's. He has so much of the information we need," Amelie said.

"Fine," she agreed, to appease Amelie and to get the conversation over with. "We'll set up a time by phone when *both* of us can come in for a consultation."

"Just call my office—" he handed Amelie his card "—and tell them you'll need a couple of hours."

"It's been a long day. I'm going home," Regina said.

"I can walk you both out," Nigel offered.

He and Amelie followed Regina out to the parking lot.

"What about you, Ms. Richards? Would you be up for an early dinner? We can talk more about the application process."

Regina gave Amelie a look, but Amelie clearly wasn't paying her any mind.

"Yes, that would be great. Regina, are you sure you won't come?"

"I'm sure."

"We'll set up a consultation time over dinner and let you know," Nigel said. "I'll just be a few more minutes, Ms. Richards, if you can wait. I have to make sure that the speakers have gotten off and that the cleanup is just about over."

"My car is over there."

"I'll be right back."

Regina headed toward her car. Nigel turned to her as she opened her door and put his hand on the small of her back.

"It'll be all right, Reggie. I know it's a lot, but you've already done most of it."

From the tone of his voice, she could tell that the hand on her back was meant to console her. It also sent a shiver up her spine. Heat flooded her middle. She hoped he couldn't tell and tried to figure out how to get him to remove his hand.

"I know. I'm just tired."

"I'm only going out with Ms. Richards to give her more information, Reggie. She doesn't know as much as you do. You're the one who's been doing the work. We'll set up a consultation time."

"I'm not worried about you going out with Amelie. I have no claim on you."

"But you do. You just don't know it." He shook his head and seemed to clear his thoughts. "But I didn't mean to say that. I just want to help you."

"You've been helpful already. I have to go."

She almost expected him to kiss her, but he didn't.

"Reggie, have a good night."

As Regina backed out of her space, she saw Nigel heading back into the building. She wasn't pleased that Nigel and Amelie were going out to dinner. He could say things about her past that she didn't necessarily want her friend to know—things that should come from her, if at all. But there was nothing she could do about that, so she might as well not worry. She didn't like the idea of involving Nigel even more in their affairs, but she had agreed to the consultation, and in all likelihood, they needed it.

She needed to stick to her real priorities and focus on the future. The next thing they needed was a new studio space.

Regina exhaled and let her shoulders droop. She hadn't realized she'd been holding her breath and steeling her back and shoulders. The slump gave her relief from the stress of the day. But she could still feel the tingling at the small of her back where Nigel's hand had been, and heat still flowed to the pit of her stomach from that brief touch. It had always been that way for them.

Chapter 10

Nigel stood in his office going over the copies he'd marked up. He'd gotten Amelie to give him her set of paperwork after dinner, which turned out to be just what he needed to get his plans under way. As before, she was full of information that Regina refused to give him, and as he had seen at the seminar, she was more than willing to take up his offer of assistance, especially once he explained that he was in love with Regina and that no strings were attached. He just wanted to help her.

The women were coming at four-thirty, and they were his last clients for that day, so he could take as much time as he needed with them. They'd need at least two hours, but whenever they finished, he could call it an early day and take them to dinner.

His secretary buzzed him at four-twenty to let him know that they had arrived. Perfect timing. He had just finished reviewing the notes he had for them. He went to call them from the waiting area himself and found Regina beautiful as ever, wearing a light yellow mid-thigh-length sundress. Something about the dress and the way it allowed the air access to her body made her seem vulnerable, fragile. He longed to touch all the places the dress would allow and had to pull his thoughts back to the work at hand.

Amelie was standing next to her in an African-print pantsuit with her braids coiled in a crown at the top of her head. Nigel nodded to her as he pulled his mind out of the gutter and motioned both women into his office and toward a small conference table.

"Welcome, both of you. Come sit over here. I set the chairs up over here so that we can all go over the draft I've marked up at the same time. It'll take a little while, but when it's over, you'll know exactly what to do to have a draft that we can send around for more commentary and then submit."

He looked at Regina to see if her spirits were still down, but her features were neutral. He put a hand on her shoulder.

"Reggie, when we're done, this will work."

"Okay."

"Let's do it," Amelie said, more enthused.

"One thing before we start the walk-through. Can we change the figure of the money you have to put up? I know you don't have a lot because you were putting a lot into renovations at the old place, but this figure is fairly low. Have you thought about outside investors? Individuals? Corporate?"

The women looked at one another and shook their heads no.

"How about me? I can put up—"

"No." Regina cut him off. "No way, no how. That just leaves us with two bills to pay instead of one."

"But I—"

"No."

Regina was adamant. Amelie just shook her head, conceding.

"Okay, but know that I'm here if you change your mind."

Nigel didn't like it, but he let it go. "You have a few other accounting calculations that need to be done. Is it all right if I do those?"

"Hallelujah," Amelie sang out loud.

Regina chuckled at that. She probably echoed the sentiment but wouldn't let herself say it out loud. Her suppressed laugh said it all. Then she caught herself and glanced at Nigel, seeming to feel awkward, as though her weakness had been found out.

Nigel had noticed. "It's okay, really. It's one of the reasons people hire accountants for this stuff, and I have all the software to do the layout." He made his voice as comforting as possible. He was trying to make sure that she didn't feel foolish.

"That done, let's walk through the marked copy," he said. Regina took out a pad and pencil. "You don't need to take separate notes. I'll give you this copy so that you can make changes. Write any clarification you need right on this so that all the notes are in one place."

Regina looked at him. They would all be looking over the same pages, and it meant that she would have to lean closer to him to take notes. He saw her weighing the threat of being closer to him in her mind.

"Okay," she said softly, and they looked at one another, a charge between them.

But Amelie was there. He ignored the electricity he felt and stifled the desire to pull her against his chest so that they could read the pages as one body. He continued on.

"A lot of my notes on the plan have to do with wording, but one of the new things you need is a section on risks."

They spent the next couple of hours walking through his copious notes and comments, and when he was done, the women had a good bit of work to do, but they knew what was needed.

"If you can do another draft of this with those changes, we'll be in business. If you'll do that and send it to me electronically, I can add the changes to the financials and go over it one more time before we hand it off to some of my colleagues for commentary. By the time you submit it, it'll be airtight."

"Except for a location," Regina said.

She looked wistful for a moment and then sighed. Nigel and Amelie exchanged glances.

"That will come," Nigel said finally. "How long do you think it will take you to get the new info, add the new sections and make changes?"

Amelie looked at Regina since it was clear that Regina would lead the brigade.

Regina looked at him, uncertain.

"At two to three hours a day, how long should it take me?"

He didn't want to underestimate and make her feel inadequate. "Two or three weeks, I'd think."

"This isn't my field, so let's say three."

He fished in his pocket and gave her another card. "Email it to me as soon as you're done, and then the three of us can meet again. Oh, one last thing. Your website. I took a look at it, and it seems dated. It doesn't show all the things that you had in the studio. I don't recall seeing mention of your classes or your credentials either."

"I know," Regina said. "We planned to update it."

"And change the name," Amelie added.

"But now we need a new address and class schedule, as well."

"Get it updated now," Nigel suggested. "Leave the old address for now, and add a projected class schedule for the fall. You can always change the address later. Even shopping the proposal around, people will want to see the website, so pretend that you're still at the old location, and update. Change the name, remove the old picture of the location, add more pictures of the pieces, a photo of a class in progress, all of that. Can you afford it, or—"

"Yes. Don't ask," Regina said.

Nigel hung his head, caught offering to help again.

"How about dinner together?" he ventured.

"It's after eight. I have to get home," Regina said quickly.

"Unfortunately, so do I." Amelie had real regret in her voice.

He hadn't noticed the time, only the electric pull he felt toward Regina. He had been close enough to smell her perfume, and his whole body had reoriented toward her center. Lost in the prospect of her future, the hours had skipped by.

The next few weeks couldn't go by quickly enough and didn't go by quickly at all. He had no real reason to contact Regina, but he called anyway, just to ask how things were going. She was polite but didn't engage him in anything other than brief talk about the paperwork.

The three were set to meet on a Friday evening three weeks later, and he'd gotten the electronic version of the updated draft that Regina had emailed. He pored over it for two evenings, correcting new issues that arose in revision, finding things that had gone unnoted the first time around and playing with the layout using his software so that it would look professionally done.

When he opened the door to his office to invite the women in, he found Regina by herself. She wore a lavender peasant blouse made of lace, and the matching crinkle peasant skirt was trimmed with lace at the hem. Her one-inch silver sandals made her seem ready for an evening out, and the whole composition seemed designed to inundate him. Simple as it was, it made him want to take her in his arms.

Focus, he told himself.

He motioned Regina in and looked about for Amelie. "Restroom?"

"Restless is more like it."

"What?"

"She had a date—of all things—and flaked out at the last minute. This is our future we're talking about. That woman can be one hot mess. She says he's a 'visitor' from out of town and is only here until tomorrow morning. But I know it's a booty call."

Nigel chuckled.

Regina continued, "She begged off, and I let her get away with it because she really chipped in with this leg of the work."

"She knows that you're the one who really knows what's going on. She can afford to be absent."

She dismissed his statement and walked toward the conference table. Her step was hesitant. Without Amelie, she had no buffer, and she was clearly less at ease. He hated that and set about to change it.

"Well, it's the same process as last time, but it won't take as long. I'm sorry about the late hour. I didn't have an opening before five, and since this is pro bono, I didn't want to cut in too much on the company's time."

"Oh, no. No problem. We understand."

"I won't have you here as late as last time, and there are still a bunch of people here. Many of our clients need to come after business hours."

"I could see that. I'm not being skittish."

"Good, have a seat. I have few changes for the proposal. Most of what I have is for the loan-application packet. Amelie gave me all of her copies, so I was able to look through everything."

He flipped opened the first folder and then had a thought.

"Hey, let's just make changes now right on the computer, at least for all of the items that aren't scanned. We can start here with things that will need to be changed at home and then move to my desk."

"Okay."

He started going through the changes, and they drew together, Regina bending toward him to make additional notes for her own clarification.

Her hand was inches from his on the table, and he absentmindedly found himself touching her fingers as he flipped through pages and folders. He didn't notice it until a strong shiver ran through her body.

"Are you cold? Should I turn down the AC?"

"No," she said, pulling her hand away.

That's when he noticed what he'd been doing. And knowing that her body had reacted to it sent heat into the pit of his stomach, made him want to do it more. But he took hold of himself and tried to control his mind. It was his lack of self-control that had widened the rift between them before, and he knew that if he chased her off again, she would walk out now and never come back—not even with Amelie.

When they were done with the scanned items, they

An Important Message from the Publisher

Dear Reader,

Because you've chosen to read one of our fine novels, I'd like to say "thank you"! And, as a special way to say thank you, I'm offering to send you two more Kimani™ Romance novels and two surprise gifts— absolutely FREE! These books will keep it real with true-to-life African American characters that turn up the heat and sizzle with passion.

Please enjoy the free books and gifts with our compliments...

Glenda Howard
For Kimani Press™

Peel off Seal and Place Inside...

EDITOR'S FREE GIFTS SEAL THANK YOU

We'd like to send you two free books to introduce you to Kimani™ Romance books. These novels feature strong, sexy women, and African-American heroes that are charming, loving and true. Our authors fill each page with exceptional dialogue, exciting plot twists, and enough sizzling romance to keep you riveted until the very end!

KIMANI ROMANCE...LOVE'S ULTIMATE DESTINATION

Your two books have combined cover price of $12.50 in the U.S. or $14.50 in Canada, but are yours **FREE!**

We'll even send you two wonderful surprise gifts. You can't lose!

2 FREE BONUS GIFTS!

We'll send you two wonderful surprise gifts (worth about $10) absolutely FREE, just for giving KIMANI™ ROMANCE books a try! Don't miss out—MAIL THE REPLY CARD TODAY!

Visit us online at www.ReaderService.com

stacked up the folders and moved to his desk, chairs together behind his computer, with her at the keyboard. He continued walking her through suggestions and changes, as both bent toward the screen.

"No," he said at one point, catching an error. "These figures should match the ones in Exhibit G, the equipment or non-real-estate assets to be purchased. And I don't recall them being..."

As he leaned over her to reach the file with the exhibits, Nigel brushed against Regina's breast. Her chest leapt forward, and a heavy shudder ran over her body. She sucked in a trembling breath, and her eyes fluttered. Good God, she was so responsive tonight.

Nigel couldn't help himself. He forgot the folder, bent toward her, and brought her lips to his, moving his hand back to her chest, which heaved against it. Her mouth opened and he moved his tongue into her moist heat, opening his palm to rake her nipples with his fingertips. And he couldn't stop.

Every tremor of her body made his manhood rage. When her hand came up to his nearest shoulder, he spun around in his seat to better position himself in front of her, all the while rubbing her rigid nipples through the thin lace of her blouse.

He moved his tongue farther into Regina's mouth, wanting more. She grabbed his neck and pulled his face closer to hers, her chest still leaping. She moaned softly into his mouth, and his manhood leapt in response.

He finally stood, pulling her up with him and into his arms where he could press her body into his, into the parts of him that had been longing to feel her. Her arms came around his neck, and his hand moved up and down her back.

He tugged her skirt upward until he could put his foot

between her feet, settling his thigh between her legs. He kneaded her buttocks with one of his hands until he felt her hips tilt forward, grinding the center of her womanhood against his thigh. She moaned again.

He had never had such strong desire to take a woman, and he might have ripped off her clothes and lifted her onto his body right there had he not been aware that the door was unlocked and had he not been certain that the gesture would send her bolting.

He pulled his head up, separating his mouth from hers.

"Reggie, come home with me. Let me make love to you. I want you so badly."

Before she could respond, his mouth found hers again. They began to kiss again, but then her hand came up between them, and she stepped back, shaking her head and taking deep breaths.

"I can't. I didn't come here to—"

Nigel inhaled slowly and exhaled.

"I'm sorry, Reggie. I don't know what hit me. It was just that you seemed so… You seemed to respond. I won't do anything like this if it means I can't help you. I'm not doing this to seduce you into being with me or anything like that. Here, sit. Let's finish."

She sat down, still breathing heavily. "Okay. Let's finish."

Nigel sat back down as well, trying to force his pulse to calm and his body to quiet. After the heat of the exchange between them, he wanted nothing more than to gather up their things and take her home. His disappointment was matched only by his determination to be of real help. That's what allowed him to regain his focus and apply it to the work at hand.

They went through the rest of the changes quickly and quietly.

"These are finished," he said when they were done.

"What about the address? I haven't changed it."

"Leave the address. There will be one there, so let's leave this one where it is for now. Oh, what about the website?"

"It will be finished next week."

"Good."

He hadn't expected it to be done that quickly, but the timing was perfect for his plans. He printed them both copies.

"Here. This draft is good. Sign these."

"They're still drafts. Amelie isn't here."

"We want them to be as complete as possible, even to show around. But we can get Amelie's signature later."

"Okay," she said, and picked up a pen from his desk.

"Once you scan the rest of the pages and get them to me, I'll make a couple of copies and hand them around. A few items will change when the location changes, but this is enough to get more feedback before the final submission. Just so you know, it can take a few weeks to get feedback. Industry people are pretty busy, and I'm not just getting this to my friends. I'll get it to the right people, not the ones who'll get it back in a couple days as a favor."

"You do that, and I'll work on the space."

Regina started packing up.

"Nigel."

"Yes, Reggie."

"I've had a few minutes to think."

She turned to him, and he could see that she had gotten serious. She had a determined look on her face, and her fist tightened around the handle of her satchel. She met his eyes with a fixed regard.

"After what just happened, I don't think we should see each other anymore," she said. "If we need to meet once more when you get the commentary back, it can be with Amelie."

"Reggie, I told you. I won't do anything to jeopardize helping you. There aren't any strings attached here. This is part of what I do. Let me help."

"I just don't want to keep sending you mixed signals."

Her signal wasn't mixed at all. He knew that she wanted him. Right from the top of her head to her little pinky toe, she wanted him. But her mind didn't want him.

And right now, it was more important to help her with this than to pursue anything else that might chase her away. She was right. This was her future that they were talking about. She wanted to do this; it was her dream. And he wanted to help her have her dream.

He decided to let it go.

"Okay. Send me the other files. When I get those, I'll send them around. We can decide later who I meet with, and it will be all three of us or just me and Amelie."

"It can be just—"

"If there are changes she won't understand, then the three of us can meet in a bright public space. If there are only minor revisions, I'll convey them to you through her. You'll be making them. That I know."

"I'm sorry for the confusion, Nigel. That's why it's better this way."

Dinner was out of the question, of course. He walked her to the elevator and watched as she got on.

The elevator closed. It closed with him not knowing when he would see her again, when he could touch her again. But he wouldn't worry about that now. He would have a long time to worry about that in the coming weeks.

Nigel went back to his office. First things first. First he had to get her business back. Then he had to try to get her back.

Chapter 11

It was some weeks later that Regina, glancing up from her plate of smoked salmon at a restaurant, saw Nigel again.

He was wearing a gray pinstriped three-piece suit and looked as professionally manicured as ever. Next to him was a tall woman, almost as tall as he was, wearing a form-fitting purple evening gown with sequins over the top. It was sleeveless and had a low cut in the front, coming down to the cusps of her ample breasts. She had her hands wrapped around Nigel's arm, and he was guiding her down the steps to the main dining floor.

Given her proportions, she was a perfect Black Barbie and probably as brainless, too—a fitting match for a successful young accountant-investor. But why was Regina being critical of the woman? She was glad that Nigel was getting on with his life the same way she was finally getting on with hers.

It was the opening night of a new jazz restaurant in

downtown DC called The Jay Birds, and Regina had finally kept her promise to herself to get a life. She was out
on the town.

Nigel caught her gaze as he looked over the dining floor
and held it long enough to notice the date seated across
from her. Regina's face flushed, and she turned back to
her dinner partner. But the intrigue made her glance back
in time to see the couple be seated, with Nigel getting a
chair that gave him a plain view of her.

She watched as the woman said something, palming Nigel's chest and shoulder before settling back in her chair.
When he looked up and caught her watching, Regina
turned her attention back to her date. He was a medical
technician at the George Washington University Hospital. He was also some distant relation of Ellison, who had
set them up.

The evening was young, but she and her date had already exhausted the topics they seemed to have in com-
mon. They inspected their plates quietly. Of course, now
that the seven-piece jazz band had started up, it wasn't
really possible to talk on the main dining floor. It was better to watch as people on the lower level, a dance floor,
moved to the band.

The music was good, and Regina couldn't help sway-
ing to it now and again. So far, it was the best part of the
evening. If she got no other pleasure out of the night, she
would at least have the joy of listening to the band—The
Jay Birds, she assumed—do classic jazz and do it the right
way.

Whenever she dared glance his way, the woman's hands
were somewhere on Nigel, and Nigel's eyes were on Regina. He was probably wondering if he should say hello.
He could spare himself the worry.

She made sure not to look over very often but couldn't

help having her attention drawn that way when three bois-
terous men and a woman stopped at Nigel's table, greeting him and his guest in loud voices and carrying on a
conversation above the music. Once again, she found his
eyes shift to her.

When they were finished with dinner, Regina and her
date turned their chairs toward the band and enjoyed the
music. He wasn't much for dancing—didn't know how to
dance to jazz, he said—so they sat and watched the danc-
ers. The music was energetic, but it didn't seem to move
him. His stillness and his plastic features made him seem
unreal to Regina.

Now that he was out of sight, she had no reason to think
about Nigel Johns, but she couldn't help wondering if he
was still glancing her way, couldn't help remembering
what had happened between them in his office. She shook
her head to free her mind of the image, then let herself become immersed in the music.

She tried not to think about Nigel again, but then he
appeared at her side, motioning toward the dance floor.
She wouldn't have given it a second thought, but the band
was playing New Orleans–style jazz, and she loved that.
She would never get a chance to dance with her date, so
she leaned over to him and shouted in his ear.

"Do you mind if I dance for a while?"

He shrugged, and she got up, moving to the dance floor
with Nigel and then kicking back to the sound.

It was pretty clear that Nigel didn't know how to move
to this music either. His awkward jerks made her laugh
out loud, but at least he was willing to try.

After a couple of songs, he found his groove and began
matching her step for step. He put one of his hands on her
hip and brought her closer, never losing a beat. A soft smile
came onto his face, and for a moment, she thought that he

might do more, but he didn't. He just moved with her, his eyes trained on her face.

If he wanted to say something, he had no chance. The music was just too loud. When the set was over, they both turned, heading back to their tables. She figured that he needed to get back to his date, and she might as well get back to hers. Her date didn't seem to be enjoying too much of this, so it was about time for them to go—either somewhere else or home, she didn't know. If she had her vote, it would be home.

Nigel couldn't keep his eyes off Regina.

When his date, Laurie, started talking with the owners, he slipped over and asked her to dance. Laurie was a networker and would spend a while working the bar area where the owners were stationed for opening night. She was the sister of one of his coworkers and only needed someone well dressed to show off for opening night. He was there because he'd helped the owner get the loan to start the place and was his accountant; he was expected. But after he'd shown his face, he planned to leave.

Regina had on a simple dress rather than an evening gown, but she looked stunning. The top part of the bodice was pleated around her torso with two little straps over her shoulders, and when she got up to dance with him, the skirt of her dress fell around the curves of her hips.

He was surprised when Regina actually agreed to dance with him, and downright shocked when she actually looked back at him—not wanting him, but not hating him. It made his heart skip a beat, made him hope that he might have a chance.

After that dance, he made sure the owner would put Laurie in a cab, made sure she knew the change in plans, and hurried to his car so that he could catch Regina leaving. He didn't personally know her date, but he had recognized him and remembered hearing that he was something of a ladies' man from mutual friends. He had to make sure that Regina got home safely. He felt like a thief or a stalker, but when they came out just as he pulled up, he followed them to their car and followed them to wherever they were going, hoping that it was her place and not his.

He was relieved to see the guy leave Regina at the curb and to see her walk up to the third story of a three-story house. Still acting on impulse, he followed her, not sure what he would say or how she would react.

Regina kicked her shoes off as soon as she hit the living room. When she heard the knock on the door, she thought that maybe her date had forgotten something. Or maybe he thought they might be continuing the evening in her apartment. If so, he was terribly mistaken.

She paused at the door, wondering what her date might be thinking and if she might have to fight off any advances. Outside of tonight, she didn't know him at all. In fact, tonight had given her no real clue either.

It was late, but she picked up her phone and dialed Amelie's number.

"Hey. If I don't call you back in ten minutes, come get me."

She opened the door with the phone in her hand and was surprised to see Nigel, not her date. "Oh."

"Disappointed?"

"Relieved. Don't ask," she said. If it had been her date, it would have been awkward, at the very least.

Actually, this should be awkward, too, but it wasn't. Somewhere in the back of her mind, she had imagined the knock on the door might be Nigel. Something about dancing with him, even in a crowded club on opening night, had made them seem like friends again. It had surprised her that he hadn't tried to talk. Maybe she had even been a little disappointed. But then, he had been on a date, as had she.

"First, once again, you should check the peephole before you open the door."

"The landing light is out. I can't see a thing out the peephole. And it's too high for me—I have to get that fixed. By the way, there is a buzzer. But you can't see it, can you?"

After the lack of conversation with her date that evening, she now felt rather chatty. She was breaking her own rules, but it was a relief to have someone around who could hold a conversation.

"And second," Nigel said, "I thought we could have a cup of coffee or…"

"Or?"

"I don't know. That's as far as I got. I only know that I had to see you."

"I'm sure—" she almost said Black Barbie "—your girlfriend wouldn't appreciate you saying that."

"She's not my girlfriend. She's my coworker's sister, who will be put in a cab by the owner, and he's the only reason I went. Business."

"I guess that doesn't let me off the hook."

She reluctantly stepped back, letting Nigel in. Part of her knew she should send him away, but the larger part of her wanted to decompress after the long night and have a real conversation with a real person.

"Okay," Regina said, "let's clear the air. I'm not putting those shoes on again, so you'll have to take whatever's in my kitchen, which is decaf, I think."

"So this is where you're living now?"

"You didn't know? My new address is on the application."

"No, I didn't get it from the application. I followed you home."

Regina made an exaggerated face, looking at Nigel like he might be a crazy stalker. He got her meaning and cracked up.

"I know. I'm a bit out there right now," he said, not wanting to tell her what he'd heard about her date. "But seeing you again... Seeing you in that dress. I don't know. Maybe it *is* time to clear the air."

"I'm in a strange mood, too. It was just one of those nights. Anyway. Clearing the air." She turned serious. "We can't go back there."

He got quiet, too. "I know. I know. But who you are now, who I am now—"

"We're different people now," she said.

"Who you are now is interesting, too. Where's your artwork?"

"I found a dealer in the art district who took pity on me and took about a third of my finished pieces on consignment. The rest is in there."

Nigel headed into the room she had pointed to.

"It's not pity. Your work is beautiful. I saw a little at the studio—I'm sorry again that you lost it. What about Amelie?"

"Oh. Amelie."

Regina still had the phone in her hand and hit Redial.

"No, you're not coming for me. It was just Nigel.... He didn't say anything about that, so I assume not." She turned to him. "Did we get any commentary back yet?" He shook his head no. "No, but I'll let you know....Oh, hush. Bye-bye." She clicked the phone shut. "Sorry about that."

"Protection?"

"Yes. That was Amelie. We have a booth on week-ends in the open market at Eastern Market. Have you been there?"

"Not yet." He was walking slowly through the room, looking at the pieces she had out front, sometimes stopping to tip a board forward and see the one behind it.

"We share a booth, but she's doing well there. Sharing it takes the pressure off the need to be there all weekend, which is nice. She has a show coming up, as well."

"She's beginning to be recognized."

"Yes. We're still trying for a place of our own."

"You'll be recognized soon, too."

They were in what would usually have been the second bedroom of her two-bedroom place. For her, it served as an art studio. His attention to her pieces drew her eyes to them, as well. She didn't realize he had moved behind her until he wrapped his arm around her.

"It's getting muddy again," she said, but she didn't pull away.

"I know," he answered.

They were quiet for a long moment.

Perhaps she just wanted to break the mood, but she had a playful thought. "You know, when you asked me to dance, you didn't say that you couldn't dance a lick to New Orleans jazz."

"Or any other jazz," he added.

They both chuckled.

"Thank you for trying. You caught on quickly."

"Yeah, your boyfriend didn't look like he was about to."

"Like I said, don't go there."

They chuckled again.

"Hey," he said, "where did you learn to dance to New Orleans jazz?" He said it like he should know everything about her.

"My older cousin Willie, from the Big Easy. He used to come visit us about once a year when I was little."

Regina moved to break the spell between them and return them to reality, but he held on to her. From behind her, he crossed his arms over her chest and rubbed her arms. The movement dragged his forearms gently over her breasts, and her body started to tingle. His mouth was near her ear, close enough that his warm breath sent shivers through her.

"You dance well. I don't dance anymore at all."

"You? The eternal partier? You're just out of practice."

"That I am."

He pointed to one of her pieces. "What do you call that one?"

She stirred slightly at his question, but he gently held her back to his chest, and rubbed her arms again. The name that had been on the tip of her tongue slipped out of her mind.

"Um. Oh, it's called *The Overlook.* See the way the figure is overlooking the horizon?"

"Yes," he said into her loose hair. He drew one of his hands around her waist and drew the other to her breast, gently caressing it through the pleats of her dress. Her body tensed, and goose bumps ran up her spine.

"Tell me about that one."

"That one is called *The Crucible.* It's a Georgia O'Keefe–type theme. Women's sexuality."

Nigel lifted his head. "Where?"

"See, there are the lips, the V for the hair. It's abstract."

"I see it now. It's beautiful. I wouldn't have gotten it if you hadn't told me."

He moved the hand on her waist down to her thighs and drew his palm up toward her V. Her buttocks contracted involuntarily, and her thighs clenched, tilting her hips. She sucked in a breath.

"Your body wants me. I want you, too."

She stopped, exhaled.

"Let's be clear. I can't go back there. This is…" She didn't know how to finish.

"Let's just say it is what it is and leave it at that."

Nigel moved his palm down Regina's thighs again and then back up. He loved the way her body bucked against his when he did it, making him stiffen.

"You know. I haven't—" she said.

"You haven't what?"

"I haven't been with anyone other than you since high school."

Nigel was floored and broke out in a grin, which she turned her head in time to catch. She playfully elbowed him in the side.

"I'm sorry," he said. "But the truth is that I haven't been with anyone other than you all this time either. Not that I haven't had offers."

"I'm sure you have."

"And clearly you have, as well."

He still held her breast in his palm, and he ran his thumb over her nipple, feeling it stiffen, feeling her whole body sway.

"It's getting murky again, Nigel."

"No, it's not. Not really. Let's just say that we're two people who've been starved for affection and who are used to each other."

"I'm not used to you," she protested. "I'm not used to anyone."

"Well, we're more used to each other than anyone else."

"And it is what it is," she said, as if to make certain that they were on the same page.

"It is what it is," he confirmed.

"But let's not make it a habit. That's when things get murky again."

He was too busy smelling her hair to respond. When he opened his eyes and dipped his head down, she looked like she was wondering what the hell she was doing. But when he ran his hand over her breasts again, her eyes fluttered shut, and a shiver ran through her whole body.

He took her and drew into the hall, looking for her bedroom.

They went inside and faced one another next to her bed. She looked at him for a long moment and then stepped into the radius of his embrace, pressing her hands against his chest, finding his nipples and closing her fingers around them, weakening his knees.

It was his grin. It seemed to turn back time in his face, making him into the boy she had known and loved before he became the man who stood in front of her now.

And it was his touch—the way he moved his fingers over her chest and the way he moved his palm up her legs, making heat and moisture flood into her body.

Still, she had to wonder what on earth she was doing with the man who had once left her. But thinking about that didn't answer her real question. Why was her body still lit on fire by his touch? Though she hedged, in the end she knew that she wanted this as much as he did, and as long as they were both clear...

But she couldn't be clear with his fingers moving over her, his hand exploring her body. She moved her hands along his chest and let herself be lost in the sensations.

When she heard the zipper of her dress, she opened her

eyes. When she felt his fingers fluttering down her back, her body arched into his, and she began to throb. She got her hands between them and undid the buttons of his shirt, wanting to feel the warmth of his skin against hers. Then she felt her dress sliding down between them, and his head dipped down to her neck and then her breasts, as the material fell to the floor.

His mouth was hot through the fabric of her bra, turning her nipples into hard peaks. He sucked one into his mouth and wetness flooded her. Her body shivered from the touch, and she couldn't hold in the murmur that escaped her. Then his fingers moved between her legs, finding her heat. Her body jerked and a soft moan poured from her throat. She had to hold his shoulder to stop from sinking to the floor as a heavy throbbing overtook her.

She slipped his blazer and shirt from his shoulders at the same time, and he straightened, letting her undress him. The passion she saw in his face made her flush. She brought the jacket over to her chair and turned to find him stripping off his pants, along with his shoes. When he saw her undo the clip of her bra and let it slip from her torso, he stopped and stared, his manhood tugging against his shorts.

She held out her hand for his pants and laid them over the seat. Then she moved into his open arms.

His mouth covered hers, and his hard chest dragged across her breasts, making her moan again. He slipped the panties down her legs and took off his shorts before lifting her onto the bed. He stopped to put on a condom he must have taken from his clothes while undressing, and then he covered her with his body.

When his manhood grazed her center, her back arched and she murmured. But instead of moving inside her, he slid his body down the length of hers, suckling her nipples before moving lower. When his mouth found her, when the heat of it covered her, Regina moaned out loud and thrust her hips. Sensations flooded her. She clung to the bedspread and thrust against his teasing lips. And he didn't stop.

She was moaning and thrusting when his fingers found her breasts, pushing her over the edge as a wave of release shattered through her body. She cried out as the pleasure ripped through her body.

She was breathing heavily as he slid upward next to her, letting her run her hands along his body—its hardness, its curves, its thick peak. She pulled him toward her, and he followed her tug, landing between her legs.

He entered her in one slow movement, building the pressure inside of her all over again. His slow thrusts filled her. His lips captured her breath. His moan filled her mouth.

His movements spread fire through her, made her body grip on to his. But he was taking his time, making her moan, making her thrust, making her build toward the edge.

When his movements became short, hard jerks, her back arched, bringing her chest to stroke along his. She moaned and he moaned as they both tumbled over the boundary.

Chapter 12

A week later, Nigel couldn't wait to see Regina again. In fact, he wasn't going to wait. And he wasn't going to follow the little rules she'd laid out for them; she could never be just a warm body to him. He had already decided to drop in on her and see what she was up to. Where it went from there, well, that was up to her.

Nigel knocked on Regina's door for the second time. When he still didn't get an answer, he remembered that there was a buzzer and decided to try it before giving up.

He heard a chain sliding, and then the door opened.

"Yes. I did look out the peephole this time, thank you."

"I didn't say a thing."

She eyed him. "You were thinking it."

He gave her an innocent face and shook his head. She laughed.

"What are you doing here? And don't you know that I

have a phone? You can call ahead. You know, I'm usually at our booth in Eastern Market by now."

"I figured, but I thought I would take a chance."

He followed her into the living room and took a seat. She was wearing jeans with a tank top and had sneakers in her hand. He loved seeing her in casual clothes almost as much as he had loved seeing her in business attire. The tank top left her shoulders out, and already his lips were itching to kiss them. In fact, he wanted to play with all of her curves.

She sat down to put on her sneakers.

"I actually do have quite a bit to get done," she said. "I can't stop and play."

"So what are we doing today?"

"Nothing in those clothes."

He wasn't ready for her to say that. He imagined that she might turn him down altogether, not that she would have an issue with his clothes.

"Don't you have any casual wear? Jeans?"

Nigel looked down at himself, perturbed.

"I think I have some jeans at home. I know I have sweat pants."

"Jeans are better," she said. "Sweat pants will do."

"Why? What are we doing today?"

"Errands."

"Errands?"

"You'll see."

At least she was amenable to the company.

They headed out as if they were used to being together. They left his car on her street, and she followed his directions to his place so he could change. Nigel liked the new feeling of being out with her, doing things, but she had never been to his place, and now he wasn't sure what she would make of it.

He let her go in ahead of him and watched her as she took it all in: a winding black leather sectional, a fully stocked cherry wood entertainment center with a six-foot coffee table and matching chest, a deep-piled eggshell carpet.

"Damn," she said.

"I actually had a decorator do it. I wanted to impress you."

"You're kidding, right?"

He sighed, realizing too late that he had perhaps admitted too much. "No, I wanted to show you that I'd made it after all."

She walked to the end of the living room and back, then turned into the hallway and found his equally decked-out bedroom. He liked the idea of having her in his room and followed her in.

"This isn't necessarily what I think of when I think of making it." She'd found his closet.

"I know. I— You seemed so certain that I would waste my life. I wanted to—"

"I wasn't certain of any such thing. I was waiting for you to…just take things a little more seriously, not ditch all the casual clothes you own." She'd been rifling in his closet, then his drawers. "Here. Let's have you try these on."

She handed him a pair of unworn jeans that still had the tags on them and a similarly new Janet Jackson T-shirt. He laughed at the tee but started stripping anyway.

"See, I do have casual clothes."

"Yes, but you've never worn them. How come?"

"I thought I needed to get rid of my old life." He shook his head, remembering the days he refused to wear anything that didn't look gangsta. "I needed to change my life around—finish school, make it in the world, prove that I could be what you needed. I guess I went to the other extreme, but it got me here. It got me to change, and I haven't looked back."

"It doesn't have to be one or the other."

"At that time, for me, it did. Now, maybe not."

When he was finished, she sized him up and apparently approved.

"Okay, let's get to it."

The first stop turned out to be a huge hardware store out in Maryland. This was Regina's element, and he followed her around while she handed him things to put in their cart—dusty ceramic tiles, powdery grout bags, tubs of mastic, cylinders of sealant, cans of paint, tubes of epoxy. Now he knew why casual clothes were needed.

"I miss teaching my classes," she mused.

"Were they adults or children?"

"Adults or teens mostly for the found-object mosaics. I can do clay work with littler ones, but the other stuff is too sharp and dangerous for them."

"You'll have a classroom back again soon."

"I know. And I'm looking for other places I can teach in the meantime."

She spent a while in the molding aisle and then pointed at a bunch of eight-foot-long molding pieces and at the cart with the handsaw.

"Make yourself useful," she said, then smiled.

"You want me to?"

"Cut them in half so they'll fit in the car. Here, I'll start them for you." She brought him over to the cart, laughing. He pulled a few pieces of the molding from the shelf and joined her.

He never knew the sight of a woman with a handsaw could be so sexy. She laid two of the pieces on the cart and measured to find the center. He didn't need to, but he got behind her to see what she was doing, fitting his thumbs into the belt loops of her jeans. He couldn't resist pulling her against him and running his cheek over her hair.

She laughed and tried to wiggle away.

"You're not looking at what I'm doing," she said, but as she turned toward him, he caught her lips with his.

They parted for him, and he turned her body toward him, pulling her into his embrace. He had to tear himself from her before he got lost in the moment.

"Okay, I got distracted. Show me again," he said.

She pursed her lips at him, turned back to the cart and started a notch in the molding. He finished them up in no time but not without a naughty picture in his mind.

A question occurred to him as they continued shopping. These supplies were going to cost a bit.

"Do you have enough coming in from Eastern Market and the art dealer?"

"That's a very private question. Actually, you've seen all my financials. You know I have a morning job, right?"

"Oh, yeah. Does it help you out enough?"

"It pays okay. I don't do a lot of hours, though. For now it gives me rent and health insurance."

"What is it?"

"It's just office work with an architectural firm in downtown DC. Nothing special. But it helps with the bills."

Next was the plywood section. This time she had the store cut down sections of large boards for her, the sawdust flying from the circular saw.

"What about you? Do you like your work?"

He was surprised by the question.

"Yes, I do. I think I started it just for the money. But I really love what I do. Some things are a little tedious—crunching numbers sometimes—but most of it I love."

"Like what?"

"Like helping people get a business going. You and Amelie, for example. Or seeing it grow. Being able to teach people more about business rather than just adding up numbers for them. Being able to guide people through the process rather than just handing them balance sheets. Helping people figure out how to save and grow money."

He stopped. It seemed to him that he'd started rambling.

"Don't stop. I like to hear you get passionate."

He hoped she did, because he wanted to get passionate with her. He dragged his mind from the gutter.

After the hardware store, they went to a tile shop. After that it was an art supply store, where Regina needed clay and slip.

"I tried the non-firing clay. It wasn't strong enough."

"Where's your kiln now?"

"It's in the workroom in my apartment. Didn't you notice it when you were in there?"

"No, I was looking at your art and at you." He dipped his head down and kissed her. Then he wrapped his arm around her as they continued through the store. The clay and slip were both incredibly heavy.

"How do you get this by yourself?"

"I'm not by myself."

"But when you are?"

"One case at a time."

Since they were in the area, they stopped at the pet store. He was thinking of a dog. They played with the puppies, looked at the fish and petted the hamsters. It was a riot.

In fact, Nigel found himself laughing on and off all day, something he didn't do a lot of anymore. As they unloaded her hatchback later that afternoon, Nigel paused and looked at her for a long moment.

"I haven't had this much fun in years."

"And you're not in a business suit. See? Success doesn't mean being all business all the time."

"And it doesn't mean that you have to do everything on your own all the time either."

Regina stopped for a minute and put her hand up to disagree but then seemed to think the better of it.

"Okay. Maybe. In fact, here."

She handed him two boxes of clay, and he started laughing.

"I don't just mean the heavy stuff. You know, I might be able to help you as well, help fund your art…"

She had already started shaking her head.

"…or help you find a new place or help you get the down payment. You don't have to be all business all the time either."

"I don't need that kind of help, but thank you."

They got everything up the stairs to her apartment and had to sit down for a minute.

"You know," he said, "you're probably exceeding the weight limit for that room."

"Hopefully it's a sturdy house. I took this place because it had the two large rooms, and that one can handle the wattage of the kiln. I have to pay for it, but I can still do my work. Luckily, I have another big installation I'm working on."

He could see how much it mattered to her.

"Come to me," he said.

"What?"

"Come here."

"Why?" she asked, but she came to him anyway.

Nigel pulled Regina onto his lap and settled back onto the sofa, massaging her back.

"That's nice."

Moments later, she started to giggle and squirm, making him laugh. This woman lit up his world.

"Not there," she squealed.

"Oh, you're ticklish here. What if…"

He did it again and she tried to get away, but he held her. He had to kiss that spot, and he lifted her tank top before toppling her forward on the couch. He kissed her back until he found the spot again. He could tell when she squirmed. Only this time when her body arched, she also murmured.

Regina's response to the touch of his lips set Nigel's body on fire. He could finally touch her without worrying that he might drive her away. She was finally his to have, to please. He opened his mouth and ran his tongue along the spot he'd found, and he was rewarded by the heavy shudder of her body and a soft moan. He lowered his torso on her thighs and continued the pressure, reaching underneath her to find a full, firm breast. Regina's breathing quickened, and her hips swirled beneath him.

It was early in the evening, but he was going to make it a long night.

Chapter 13

Regina pulled her eyelet camisole over her head, stepped into her leggings, brushed her hair into a ponytail and slipped into her sandals. She didn't have time for anything else.

The times she'd been with Nigel were all impromptu—him stopping by to see her. She'd helped to make it that way—keeping things casual so that he wouldn't get the wrong idea, keeping the pressure off so that things between them wouldn't escalate. This was a little different. They had spoken by phone in advance. They were going to look at possible new locations for the studio. Since he was closer to the first stop, she would meet him at his place. Yes, this was different.

She was implying that it was okay for them to hang out together. Maybe it was, as long as things were clear between them. The times they'd been together had felt good. And she had to admit that it felt great having some attention to her…well, womanly needs. As long as that was all it was; as long as they both knew that it was what it was.

She rang his buzzer, and he let her into his building.

The door to his apartment was open, and he called to her from the bedroom.

"Sorry I'm a bit late. Damn, it's early in the morning."

"I have seven places to see and one day to do it."

"I know. I'll be right there."

Nigel came out of his room wearing only his boxers. She could see the muscular ridges of his chest and the rugged curves of his arms. He looked like a chocolate statue—good enough to eat. He put a cup of coffee in the kitchen and came back to kiss her, a light peck on the lips. She pulled him back and ran her fingers over his chest, kissing him again. Definitely good enough to eat.

As long as everything was clear between them.

He stayed beneath her touch and looked at her.

"You know, we could see places another day. And if you keep touching me this way, we might have to."

She slipped her arms around him. "I'm just a bit randy today."

"Oh, hell."

She laughed when he picked her up and strode into his bedroom.

"No, no. We don't have time for this. I have to see the places."

He gave her a crestfallen look, placed her on the bed and pulled his shirt off the hanger.

What had gotten into her? She took a breath and tried to focus on the property search.

The first location was in DC but too far from downtown to be inviting and more broken-down than their old place was. There was no place for a classroom setting, and there was peeling woodwork, rodent droppings and little visibility from the street. They could afford the rent, but it would drive them into bankruptcy.

"Let's go. We can't attract clients from here. It would take more than we can get to fix it up."

"They'll get better, Reggie. Don't worry."

The next location was actually in the art district. It had recently been vacated by a silversmith and still had the jewelry display cases. It didn't have a separate class space, but it was big enough to improvise, with large storefront windows and the jeweler's shelving. It was clean and white and looked new. It was also out of their price range—way out. The jeweler had probably gone out of business trying to make the rent.

"I couldn't price my work high enough to keep this place."

They went on to the next two locations, then the next three. It was the same story. They were either crap that was affordable or nice but too expensive to keep up. The whole day was wasted.

"We'll keep looking, Reggie. There'll be something soon."

Regina looked through her papers at the listings she'd found and all the leads the real estate agent had given her to try to find something else they might go see. Nothing. She threw them all into a garbage can on the way back to the car. What next? They were looking in DC, Maryland and Virginia. Maybe they were in the wrong states. She could widen her search. Damn it. How did other businesses make it?

"What are you thinking?" Nigel asked as they sat together in the car.

It shook her out of her reverie. "I'm just wondering what to do next."

"You're letting it get you down. It could take a while to find the right place. Give it time."

"Right now, time is income. I've—"

She had started to say that she'd asked for more hours at her morning job, and she'd gotten them, but it meant less time to work on her art. It meant she was losing her dream. But she didn't want to say this out loud, and not to Nigel, sitting there staring at her in his designer suit. It was some reversal, wasn't it? Tears moistened her eyes, but she didn't want to cry.

"I'll keep looking," she said. "If it's meant to be, we'll find something fairly soon. If it's not, I'll take a break and start some other path."

"Reggie, trust me, please. It will be okay. And if you need anything in the meantime, I'm here."

"I know," she said. But she would never turn to him for that kind of assistance. "You know, this is why I was so serious in school."

"What?" Nigel turned to her.

"I knew it would be this hard. Or at least that it was likely to be."

"You couldn't have known that we'd have a major economic recession."

"No, but even without that, I knew that trying to live as an artist would be hard. I knew it, so I should be ready for it. Let's hope I am."

Regina started the car and headed back to his place, still down.

"Can you come in for a while?" he asked. "I'll make us something to eat."

"No, you go ahead. I have to get ready for my housewarming party tonight. You still coming?"

"I'll be there, tot in tow."

She started to pull off.

"Reggie," he called out. She slowed down and turned back to look at him. "I promise you that things will be okay. Don't let it get you down."

"I know. I won't."

But it seemed like a promise that he couldn't make.

When she got home, Regina didn't go into the kitchen to start getting ready for the evening. She got on the computer. She had to find other options, or she wouldn't be able to make it through the evening. In an hour, she had the information for another commercial real estate brokerage company in the DC area and two more sites on which to do searches. She picked an afternoon to drive around and look for open locations near the Torpedo Factory; if she'd learned anything today, it was that location was indeed everything.

She also had the name of a photographer who could take pictures of a few of her mosaics—the ones she made the tiles for herself and had soldered templates for. Those she could reproduce. Maybe she could get a Black catalogue company to advertise them or could put ads in a magazine herself. It was all worth trying.

That would have to be it for now. She was having a housewarming party that night, and she did have to get ready.

Regina had changed into an African-print summer dress and had finished preparing the food.

Jason and Ellison, along with little Kyle, were the first to arrive and brought a platter of home-broiled chicken. Nigel was the next to arrive, and as soon as he entered, he bent down and gave her a warm hello kiss.

Nigel had a little boy in one arm and a bag in the other.

She took the bag from him. She didn't know he had planned to, but he'd brought homemade pasta salad. The bag also had a wrapped present for her that turned out be a sweetgrass basket from South Carolina. "It's beautiful. And expensive. You didn't have to."

"I wanted to. I thought you'd like it."

"Oh, I love it."

Regina knew that Jason was all eyes and would want more information later. So be it. She drew Nigel into the living room and introduced him around.

"Nigel, this is Jason."

They shook hands. "I remember you from the studio. Hey," Nigel said.

"This is his partner, Ellison, and their son, Kyle."

Regina watched his response to her gay friends, but he didn't seem surprised and didn't miss a beat.

"I remember you from the studio, too," he said to Kyle, then shook Ellison's hand. He turned to the little one in his arm.

"You remember Andre from my office."

"Hello, Andre," Regina said.

Surrounded mainly by adults who were peering at him, Andre twisted on Nigel's shoulder and hid his face against it.

"He's a little shy sometimes," said Nigel. "I'm babysitting for my cousin Michelle. Say hello." Andre continued to hide his face and shook his head no. "Okay. Maybe later. Here, meet Kyle. He's little like you." Andre turned around and looked over at Kyle, held on Ellison's hip. "Maybe he wants to watch your movie with you. You want to ask him? Yeah, let's ask him."

Nigel pulled the movie out of his blazer.

"Can I put on a movie for them? I promised Andre he could see it."

He handed the DVD to Jason.

"Looks good."

"They can watch it in the corner. I'll set up a little table for them as well so that they can eat."

"Does that sound good? You hungry?" Nigel asked Andre and rubbed his tummy. Andre giggled. "I'll take that as a yes."

Regina set the kids up in front of the movie with plates and went to set things out in the kitchen now that people were starting to arrive. When she got back, the kids were glued to an animated film about robots, and the three men were engaged in a lively debate over old-school dance music. Regina didn't know much of what they were talking about, but it had Ellison off his seat, and before she knew it, the three men were doing some step from back in the day, clapping each other's backs and laughing out loud.

She raised an eyebrow in question, and the men broke out laughing again.

Nigel slid his arm around her back as she neared, still laughing. She saw Jason taking mental notes, but there was nothing she could do.

"Actually, should I put on some music?" Jason asked.

"Funkadelic," Ellison said.

"Hush, now," Jason said. "That's before your time."

"Technically, it's before all of our times," Nigel said. "It was the sampling that turned us on to all the older stuff."

"Ice Cube," they said in unison.

"You have no idea what we're talking about, do you, sweetie?" Nigel teased.

"I know Parliament Funkadelic—kind of."

The three men laughed, and she didn't mind that it was at her expense. She was glad that they were all getting on so well. She got up, put on some music and checked on the kids. When she sat down, the conversation had turned to money, finances and the economy. Knowing Jason and

Nigel, she guessed this would be another heated topic. She was glad she had to leave them to get the door.

Guests had started coming. Amelie brought a date. Little Tenisha was there, along with her parents, and she joined the boys for the movie. A couple of her coworkers from her morning job came. Several of her college friends who where still in the area stopped in. One even remembered Nigel.

"No, it isn't Nigel Johns!" Simone yelled.

The two hugged enthusiastically. Simone had been one of Regina's closest friends and knew Nigel well.

"Simone. You were my big sister. Man, I was a pain in your butt, wasn't I?"

They both laughed.

"Not all the time."

The two stepped aside to catch up.

When the movie was done, Nigel went to amuse the kids for a while, but little Andre was cranky and started to cry. Nigel gathered Andre up and placed him on his shoulder, and then came to Regina.

"I'm not an expert, but I think this one is tuckered out. I better head home."

"You can put him down in my room."

"Actually," Nigel said, "let me call his mother so she knows we're still here. Can she pick him up from here?"

"Sure."

Regina spent parts of the night next to Nigel and other parts with her other friends. Toward eleven o'clock, though, the gathering had gotten thin, and by midnight, it was as it had begun: Jason, Ellison, Nigel and Regina.

Regina got up to start loading the dishwasher when the buzzer rang.

"That'll be Michelle."

"I got it," Regina said on her way.

Regina welcomed Michelle in, got her something to eat and kept her company in the kitchen while doing some cleaning up.

"Why don't I know you from Charleston? I lived not too far from Nigel," Regina said.

"Our families weren't that close. We saw each other for weddings and funerals—that kind of thing," Michelle explained. "I was also a bit wild."

"I know what you mean."

When she was done, Michelle started helping Regina pick things up.

"Stop. You don't have to do that."

"I don't mind. Nigel really likes you. That makes you like family. You're lucky, Regina. He's a good guy."

Regina didn't know what to do with the comment, so she simply smiled.

After Michelle left with Andre, Jason and Ellison got ready to leave with Kyle. At the door, Jason bent down and whispered to her.

"We need to talk, honey. I need a major update."

He nodded toward Nigel, who was saying good-night to Ellison, and winked at her. "Overnight guest?"

Regina waved him away but smiled as Nigel and Ellison approached them.

"Nice to meet you," Nigel said to Jason, shaking his hand.

"You, too," said Jason.

When the door closed, Regina was left standing alone with Nigel.

She looked up at him.

"You want help with the rest of the cleanup?"

"Okay."

"I was worried about you after today," Nigel said.

She was doing some of the dishes in the sink, and he was wrapping up the leftovers.

"I'm over it, for now at least."

"Good. It'll be okay. Hey, we're almost done. You up for a late-night movie?"

"Like?"

"I still have the one the kids watched."

She laughed. "That sounds fun. And thank you for bringing the pasta and for the sweetgrass basket. It's perfect. You didn't have to."

"I wanted to. And I had a great time tonight."

She knew he had. He had laughed a lot, and the serious man he had become had slipped away for the night.

They curled up together on the couch and started the movie. It was strange to her—the way they were getting along. She needed to process it, figure it out, but right then, it simply felt comfortable.

"Oh, no. The robots' children are being reprogrammed," Nigel cried, and they both laughed. "What do they make for kids these days?"

"Stop. It's cute."

He rubbed her head. "Aww."

Regina found herself looking at him more than the movie, and finally she turned to simply stare. She stopped and turned her head back to the television as she reached up and ran her fingers down his face. She repositioned herself on the couch and bent toward him until her mouth was next to his ear. But she didn't say anything. She kissed his lobe and ran her tongue along the inside of his ear.

Nigel got still for a moment, but as she continued, he brought his hands to rest around her back. She wanted to turn him on. She had never wanted to turn a man on so much in her life.

"What are you doing?"

"Do you want me to stop?"

"No. Hell, no."

Regina moved down from his ear to his neck, moving her hand up to his chest. Frustrated, she pulled his shirt out of his pants and slid her hands underneath, playing with his nipples.

He moaned softly, and she felt her womanhood inflame. Turning him on was making her hot and wet, and she didn't want to stop.

She shifted herself onto him, straddling his thighs, and brought her mouth to his, gently running her lips over his before opening her mouth to him. He dragged her up his lap to sit flush against his body, but she didn't want him to be the one in control, not just yet.

When she started rocking her hips over his thighs, Nigel moaned and squeezed her waist.

"Can you feel that?" she asked.

"Yes, yes."

She unbuttoned his shirt to have freer access to his chest. Then she pulled her dress over her head and took off her bra. She ran her breasts over his chest, rocking her hips over him until the center of her heat undulated over his manhood. Then she couldn't help moaning.

Nigel moved his hand over one of her breasts, but she took it away and pressed herself back against his chest. Then Nigel moved his hand between them, using his thumb to caress her. She knew that he must feel her wetness through the thin mesh of her panties. But at that moment, such exquisite anguish filled her body that she could only cry out and oscillate against him.

She hadn't meant it to happen this way, but as his finger moved over her, it filled her body with an excruciating ache. She pulled back from him and gripped his shoulders as pleasure tore through her center. His finger continued to move over her, and she couldn't stop herself from rocking over it, from riding along his body. She couldn't stop, even knowing that he was watching her shameless gyration. As her womanhood convulsed, she cried out, shuddering as waves of contractions flowed through her center.

When her body had started to calm, she felt naked and embarrassed and looked at him to see what he was thinking. His eyes were glazed over with passion, but he must have seen her hesitation.

"That was the most erotic thing I've ever experienced," he said, looking directly in her eyes.

She smiled and kissed him, grateful.

Then she felt down between them.

"It's not over yet."

She got up from his lap and pulled him up with her. Then she took his hand and led him to the bedroom. It was late, but she was going to have her way the rest of the night.

Chapter 14

Nigel switched the phone from one ear to the other.

"I can't tonight," Regina said on the other line. "I just found out that my father's having surgery. They didn't tell me because they didn't want to worry me with all that I have on my plate right now. But it's major surgery, and it's tomorrow. My aunt, his sister, has already flown in from Charleston to New Jersey. I can't take my car, and the last Amtrak train leaves at ten o'clock, which I can't make. Maybe I should just take my car."

"Slow down. What's going on?"

Regina took a breath that was audible over the line. "I'm sorry. I didn't mean to unload on you. I'm just a bit frantic right now."

"Why can't you drive?"

"I've been having minor trouble with my car. A pinging sound that comes and goes, trouble starting sometimes. I don't trust it before the next tune-up."

"I'll drive you."

"You have to work tomorrow."

"I can get back in time. I'm checking driving times on-line right now. What time do you want to leave?"

"It's almost nine now. How about ten, when the train leaves? I can't make it to the station, but I can be ready by then."

"Have you eaten?"

"Yes."

"I'll get a snack for myself on the way and see you at ten. It takes three and a half hours to get to Trenton. It's a straight shot on I-95. We'll make it fine, and I'll be back in time for work."

"You'll be up all night."

"I'll be fine. I'll see you at ten."

Nigel changed out of his good suit, stopped for a sandwich at a convenience store and headed over to Regina's early. He ate on the couch while she called her mom, started packing, called work and left a message, emailed her boss, called Amelie about the booth at Eastern Market over the weekend, finished packing and changed. It was nine forty-five when she was done with everything and sat down to fidget. He ate his late dinner knowing that his main job was to simply be there and to stay out of the way.

"If you're ready, let's leave early so you can get some sleep when you get there," he said.

"I don't think I'll be able to sleep, but we might as well go."

"Don't worry." He rubbed her shoulder. "You'll be there soon."

Along the way Nigel learned that they'd found a growth in her father's liver. Tests couldn't tell if it was malignant or benign, but the goal was to go in and get it out regardless. Regina was nervous, and he did his best to ease her tension, but all he could really do was listen and be an arm for her to rest on.

They got to Trenton just after one and to her parents' house before one-thirty. Regina's parents were asleep, but her aunt let them in. He stayed long enough to use the restroom, make sure Regina had her cell phone and say good-night.

She walked him to the door, worry written over her features.

"Try not to stress, Reggie," he said.

He pulled her into his arms, and she clung to him for a moment. He tightened his embrace and just held her.

They didn't stir until she took a deep breath and let go.

"Thank you, Nigel. This means—"

He found her mouth with his and muffled her words. He felt her open to his kiss, and when he pulled away, her arms remained wrapped around his neck.

"I'll be there for you, Reggie," he said. "I'll never let you down again."

"Thank you."

They didn't step apart until they heard Regina's aunt rustling in the kitchen. They lingered for a moment and moved together into one final hug.

"He's in good hands," Nigel said. "Don't worry."

Regina nodded, and he turned to go.

He was home in time to grab a couple hours of sleep before heading to the office.

He spoke to her a couple of times that week. The surgery had gone well, and the tumor was benign. It was relatively small, and her father would be home recovering by the end of the week.

"When should I come pick you up?"

"I can take the train back. It's not a panic like it was coming here."

"I can come pick you up. That way, I get to see you, spend a little time with you. Just tell me when."

She hesitated for a minute.

"With my aunt here and my dad doing well, I don't need to stay too long. Why don't you come on Saturday, stay over and we can leave on Sunday?"

"Do your parents have room for me, or should I find a hotel? I don't mind staying in a hotel. In fact, it would be best, with your father just home recovering."

"No. There's a den with a pullout sofa. It won't be a problem."

Now it was his turn to hesitate. "Sure?"

"Sure."

"Okay. I'll be there at noon on Saturday," he said. "That gives us time to run errands."

"See you then."

"Bye, baby."

He spent a good part of the week working on the designs he had for her application and getting more information from Amelie for his plans. As the weekend approached, he was more than ready to see her again, though he was nervous about meeting her parents after all that had happened between them. And he was right to be nervous, at least in part.

He called her just before he got there to let her know he was close. She met him at the door of her parents' home in Trenton's West Ward. They greeted each other with a brief hug, but he gritted his teeth as she led him inside.

"Mom, Aunt April, you remember Nigel."

Her mother was the one to speak.

"I don't have to think too hard after how he broke your heart."

"I know, Mom. That was a while ago."

Nigel finally found his voice. "Hello, Mrs. Gibson."

He stood near the door with his backpack, looking into the living room where the two older women were seated. Behind them was a dining set and a doorway leading to the kitchen, and off to his left were stairs leading up to the second story.

As he took in their home, Regina's mother was eyeing him up and down, making it clear that "a while ago" didn't matter. He had broken her baby's heart.

"Well, come in. Put your things down in here."

"How is Mr. Gibson doing, ma'am?"

She sighed and softened a bit. "We brought him home yesterday. Still has pain but has medication to take. They just rush folks out of the hospital these days. Soon as he could walk down the hall, they let him go. But the good thing is that the surgery went well, so he's out. Sleeping now."

"This is for him."

Nigel handed her a gift bag that held a housecoat and a toiletry set. She looked inside but didn't take anything out.

"That's thoughtful of you. We'll wait 'til he wakes before giving it to him.

"Well, Nigel Johns." She turned to face him and looked at him hard. "I ain't forgot how you tore this one to pieces." She gestured at Regina, and he swallowed hard. "But I thank you for bringing her up here Monday night and for coming to get her."

He could tell that he was being placed on warning. He'd done it once. He better not do it again, not even if he was being nice about bringing her home.

"It's no problem at all, Mrs. Gibson."

"You look like you made out okay for yourself. How're your folks? They still in the old neighborhood?"

"Yes, ma'am. They're still in Charleston in the same place. They're doing fine."

Thankfully, Regina stepped in.

"Nigel, I have some errands for us to run."

"And I need to check on your father," her mother said.

After Regina's mother went upstairs, her aunt April came out of the kitchen and offered them some iced tea.

"I remember you, too, son. You turned out good. Don't worry about Maretha too much. She'll come around."

"Thank you, ma'am."

It was thanks for both the tea and the welcoming words.

Nigel exhaled and turned to Regina. "Errands sound good."

They both chuckled.

"I'm sorry about my mom."

"Don't be. She's right to be protective of you."

"I know, but I'm still sorry."

Nigel put down his empty glass. "Let's get to those errands."

"Aunt April, when we come back, we're taking you out to dinner. Okay?"

"That'll be nice. Y'all be careful."

They picked up a few movies in the department store—a couple of Westerns for her father, a couple for them to watch that night.

"You know this city pretty well for a South Carolinian," Nigel commented.

"My parents moved here when I was in college, remember?"

"Yeah, I do now. I noticed how strong your mom's accent sounds. We don't notice it until we're somewhere up north."

Regina smiled. "I know. And notice how we've lost ours? Assimilationism."

They both chuckled.

"I hope my mom didn't put you off."

"No, don't worry about it. She has every right to be angry with me after all that happened. Did she know about…the pregnancy?"

A sternness came into Regina's face, and he almost wished he hadn't asked. "No."

The severe look on her face made him let it go, even though he wanted to say more.

"I'm sorry," she said. "It's a sore spot. But don't take my parents too much to heart. It was a bad time for me."

"I thought I knew that, but now I understand even more."

She didn't say anything else, so he let it go, and they started on their last errand.

Regina knew the city, but she didn't know the grocery store. It took them a while to complete the list, but they liked feeling that they were helping out. They also threw in a few extra items: some meats, a selection of gourmet cookies, some nutrition-boosting drinks for her father.

When they got back to her parents' house, her father was awake, and Regina went up to sit with him for a little while. After an hour or so, she called down to Nigel.

"Yes. What can I do?"

"Come up and say hello to my dad."

Nigel took a breath and climbed the steps to Regina.

"Knock and go in," she whispered.

He did. Mr. Gibson was propped up in bed with his eyes closed. He opened them to look at Nigel when he entered but then spoke with them closed.

"Come in, Nigel. Sit for a moment."

Nigel went in and took the seat next to the bed.

"Good evening, Mr. Gibson. How are you feeling?"

"I've had better days. Still sore from the surgery, but it

looks like they got everything. Took some pain medicine when I got up about two hours ago."

"I hope you feel better soon, Mr. Gibson."

"Now, what are you doing with my daughter again?"

He hadn't even tried to soften the blow. Nigel wasn't prepared for the question, but he knew he had to answer with the truth.

"I love your daughter, Mr. Gibson. She's the only woman in the world I want to be with—if she'll have me. I don't know that yet. But I want to find out."

He opened his eyes to look at Nigel for a moment and then closed them again.

"You cracked her heart open before, boy. You know what it's like to see your own child cry, and you can't do nothing about it?"

Nigel's mind went to the child that hadn't come to be, and it made the question real.

"No, sir."

"I won't let you hurt her again. Know that."

"I won't, sir. I promise."

"Good. Keep that word. A man is his word."

"Yes, sir." Mr. Gibson was quiet after that. "I'll let you rest, sir. Let me know if you need anything."

"Good night, boy."

Nigel headed downstairs. He felt like he'd been grilled again, but he also understood why. In fact, he understood why even more now. When Regina called off their wedding, to him, it was like being put out. But to her? Even though she was the one to call it off, it had hurt her in ways he hadn't understood then, and then the baby... Being here only emphasized to him the real extent of her pain.

He looked at Regina, who was sitting on the couch talking to her mother and aunt. She smiled at him as he neared. He wanted to talk to her, but it would have to wait.

They took Aunt April to dinner and then to do a little shopping downtown before the stores closed. She didn't need anything, but she wanted to get out a little bit while she was visiting her brother up north. After that they sat and talked with her mother, watched one of the movies they'd gotten and turned in.

It toyed with his urges to be sleeping in the same house with Regina when he couldn't hold her, but he also understood what it meant that she had let him come see her family and stay overnight.

The next day they let Nigel sleep in until after ten o'clock.

"You needed to get your rest, son, all this driving," Mrs. Gibson said.

"I'm usually up early. I guess I did need it."

"Here, take this up to Mr. Gibson before you head out."

"Head out?"

"We're going to get everybody brunch," Regina said.

"Hold his head while he drinks it. Then leave it on the table."

Nigel took the cup of nutritional supplement upstairs and knocked on the door before entering.

"I have a drink for you, Mr. Gibson."

"Come in."

"I'm supposed to hold your head while you drink," he said, propping the older man's head up with his hand and holding the cup to his mouth. It was a little awkward, especially after the talk they'd had the day before, but being asked to do it made him feel that they'd started to forgive him—both Regina's mother, who had asked him to do it, and her father, who allowed him to do it. "Just let me know when you've had enough."

"There. That's good. Thank you, son."

"I'll leave it here for you. Do you need anything else?"

"Find me something on the television."

Nigel sat down, found the remote and started flipping through channels, not sure where to stop.

"Here's *Law and Order*. Do you like that?"

"Not right now."

"Here's a Western. How about that?"

"That's good. Leave it there. Thank you."

"We'll be back soon, sir."

"Good."

Nigel went back downstairs to find Regina smiling at him again, and they headed out to the restaurant in his car.

"What's the smile for?" he asked.

"I'm just glad to see that my parents have mellowed out about you."

"Yeah, I guess they have. I wonder why?"

"I don't care why," she said, "as long as they stop the cold-shoulder routine."

"It's understandable."

"They should get over it."

He turned to her, seriously.

"Can *you* get over it?"

She waved the question away, but he couldn't let it go.

It came up again when they stopped for lunch on the three-and-a-half-hour ride home.

"Reggie, can we talk?"

"Yeah. What?"

He reached across the table and took her hand.

"I tried to say this before at your parent's house, but we were busy, and we couldn't just sit down and talk. I hurt you. I hurt you more than I realized. I guess I thought that because you had been the one to call things off, you couldn't be as devastated as I was. And I didn't know about losing the baby. I didn't know that I wasn't there when you were going through that. And your parents didn't know, so they weren't there. You were alone."

She sighed. "I was."

"That's why you can't forgive me. But I'm sorry. I never meant to hurt you that way. I never meant not to be there."

"I know."

"I'd do anything to make those things up to you, if I could. I just need you to know that."

"Okay," she said.

"Okay."

They finished their lunch in silence and then got back on the road.

Could she forgive him? It was the question that would determine his future, but he couldn't bring himself to ask it out loud. He couldn't face all the possible answers, especially because underneath that question was another. Could he forgive himself?

As they drove, Nigel drew her closer to his side and took her hand in his. They were quiet. With her warm body near his, all he could think was how much he loved this woman, how glad he was that she was next to him, how much he wanted to have her in his life.

Chapter 15

Regina had just finished teaching a mosaics class at the school of one of her friends, an art teacher, and she got home to find that she'd missed another call from Nigel.

Regina was beginning to worry. She had been wrong about Nigel; or rather, she had been right. She had always thought that he was smart and that he had potential. But now she was starting to get used to seeing him, starting to want to see him, and that bothered her. After their past, she had to be the stupidest person in the world for even still talking to him. She remembered his question. Could she get over it?

It was one thing when it was only physical. Now he had met her friends, had visited her folks, was getting along with everyone. And worse, she liked it that he did. It was getting muddier and muddier. She'd been ignoring his calls for a few days and was determined to put a bit of distance between them. She picked up the phone and called him back. It was time to put on the brakes.

"Hey. Can you talk, or are you still at work?"

"I'm between clients. I can talk. I need to know why you've been avoiding me, not returning my calls. What's going on? Wait, do you want to have dinner tonight and talk in person?"

"I can't. I'm seeing Jason and Elli tonight."

It wasn't an excuse. She did already have plans.

"Then tell me now. Why are you avoiding me?"

"I'm not avoiding you. I just don't want to get too dependent, too serious."

"Too serious?"

She heard the surprise in his voice.

"Yes. We've been seeing a lot of each other. I don't want it to become…"

"To become?"

She couldn't find other words at the moment, so she repeated herself.

"Too serious."

He paused for a second and then sought clarification.

"You think we've been getting too close, talking too often, seeing each other too much?"

"Yes."

He was silent. When he spoke again, his voice was softer.

"Don't you enjoy our time together?"

"Yes, maybe too much."

She regretted the words as they came out of her mouth. She had given away her own state of ambivalence and confusion. She hurriedly tried to cover her tracks.

"I don't want us to get too attached. I can't go back there, remember? I need to put on the brakes."

She heard him sigh.

"I guess things have been going pretty quickly recently. We can slow it down. Let's go out next week. How about

Thursday? I'll call you on Wednesday, and I won't nag you by phone until then. How's that?"

She didn't have a reason handy to say no.

"Okay."

"I'll get us tickets for something, and we'll have dinner. Sound good?"

"Okay."

"Reggie."

"Yes?"

"I'll have some news on the application by then. I just got one response. The news is good so far. The one we really need, though, the one who works at a bank—he needs more time. It's taking longer than I thought."

"I know. Has Amelie gotten you the last pieces of information you said you needed to update her personal finances?"

"No, she hasn't. But with this delay, it doesn't really matter."

"And with no space as yet. I'm still looking."

"I know. We can talk more next week."

"Okay."

Nigel hung up the phone. When he'd called her name, he'd wanted to say "I love you."

He'd been worried about her. Now, he was glad that she was all right, but he had to deal with her putting on "the brakes" when his body ached for her.

"Too much," she'd said. She enjoyed their time together too much. This woman loved him and didn't want to love him. Maybe he should understand it after how much she'd been hurt, but he wanted them to have passed that already. It *felt* like they were past that already.

He'd wanted to tell her again that he loved her, but instead he'd diverted their attention to the business propos-

als and loan application. He needed to give her an update
about that anyway, before she started asking. But he didn't
want that to become the only reason they saw each other.

He wanted to talk about it more.

He would see her next Thursday. Until then, he would
just have to wait.

Regina met Jason, Ellison and Kyle at a children's restaurant out in Maryland where they had planned to have
dinner and play with Kyle. She got lost on the way there
and was late, so Kyle and Ellison had already eaten, and
Kyle was already playing in a ball pit by the time she got
there. Ellison was at the side watching him and waved at
her when she came in.

"Have you eaten, too?"

"No," Jason said. "I've been waiting for you."

"Sorry I'm late."

They ordered burgers when the waitress came around,
and then Jason got down to the real talk.

"So?"

Regina sighed. She knew what he was quizzing her
about.

"So we decided to be friends."

"With benefits?" He raised a brow. He already knew
the answer.

"Well, yes."

He swallowed his bite and leaned across the table.
"What I saw wasn't just friends."

"I know. It's way out of hand. I don't actually know
what to do."

"What about what happened before? Are you over that?"

She shrugged. "I don't know."

"Do you like being with him now?"

Regina didn't want to admit it but had to. "Yes. But I

don't want it to get serious. I don't want to get back in a relationship with him."

"What I saw was already a relationship."

"I'd been ignoring his calls for a few days. It is like we're dating, but that's not what I want."

Jason was very matter-of-fact. "You want to be friends with benefits."

She shrugged. "I guess."

"And if he wants more?"

"That's the problem."

He eyed her closely. "You seem to like it when it's more."

"That's a problem, too."

Jason laughed. "Girl, you're confused."

"That's a problem, too."

They both laughed.

Then Jason got more serious. "You may not be able to have it both ways, sweetie. It sounds like you need to make a decision."

Regina sighed and toyed with her French fries. She knew that Jason was right.

Chapter 16

Nigel picked Regina up on Thursday at seven. He'd gotten them tickets for an eight o'clock show at the Arena Stage, and he'd found an all-night diner on Connecticut Avenue where they could have a late supper afterwards.

It would have been better if they could start with dinner so she wouldn't get hungry during the show, but he had to work a bit late doing the books for two companies that were merging. Regina didn't seem to mind.

She was dressed for a night at the theater when he got to her door, and she smiled at him. She seemed delighted to be going out. It wasn't what he had expected after her talk about them needing to slow down, but then, she had always been the type to get excited for a night out. He hoped she was delighted to be going out *with him*.

She had on a strapless white cocktail dress. The top was crinkled and hugged her body down to her hips. From there it flared out into a wide skirt that was covered in organza and ended above the knee. Along with that she had on a matching organza shawl and high-heeled strappy silver shoes. Her hair was piled in newly set curls on the crown of her head, with a studded barrette holding it in place. She was nothing short of a vision.

There was a slight reserve about her at first, but when she found him staring at her, speechless, she opened the shawl out behind her and twirled slowly on her heels, grinning, all reservation gone.

"You like?"

"You're gorgeous."

She laughed, made a hop. Then she just smiled.

He was still frustrated over the moratorium she'd put on their seeing one another, but in the face of her playfulness and obvious cheer, he started to forget all their troubles.

"We haven't really been out before, have we?" he asked.

She looked puzzled.

"I mean just out to have a good time, not to do something else."

She thought about it. "I guess not."

"Well, this will be good for us then. I hope you like the show."

"I will. What is it?"

He chuckled.

"You can't say you'll like it if you don't know what it is. It's called *Shooting Star*. It's a musical about a Black woman who's struggling to become a singer. I guess it's in line with *Dreamgirls*."

"Sounds good. Let's go."

He was proud to have her on his arm when they entered the theater and pleased that despite what she'd said the other day, she seemed happy to be with him. Throughout the show, he kept his arm around her, and she leaned over in her chair to nestle against him. During one of the musical numbers, they were bobbing together in unison, their heads almost touching. They looked at each other and broke out laughing. He kissed her forehead and pulled her closer.

After the show, they headed to the diner.

"I'm sorry to bring you to a diner in such a lovely gown. Most places are closed already."

"I love diners."

"Still, it doesn't fit."

"It suits me fine."

They ordered and talked about her business proposal and loan application while they were waiting for their dinners to arrive. He updated her on the feedback he was supposed to be collecting, repeating what he'd said on the phone in more detail.

Then they talked about how her search for a location was going. It hadn't gotten anywhere yet, but she hadn't given up hope. He found out that her father was recovering a little more each day and that she had taught an art class last week for a friend working at a private high school.

They talked about everything except what they most needed to talk about. He thought about broaching the subject of their relationship a dozen times. But each time, he put it aside, not wanting to disturb the warmth between them.

When they were finished, he wrapped his arm around her again, squeezed her thigh and said, "Come home with me."

"Okay."

He hadn't expected her to say yes but was elated when she did.

"But I have to be home early in the morning," she said. "I have to be at work by eight."

"Me, too."

They drove back to his apartment and settled into the living room together. He'd never spent time with her at his place before, and despite the unanswered questions that hung between them, he was thrilled to see her curled up on his sectional, her shoes discarded on the floor, her white dress standing out against the black leather, her bare shoulders calling to his lips.

He took off his jacket and slid over on the couch, positioning himself so that he could kiss her, and then he stopped.

"Can I get you something more comfortable to sleep in?"

He would love to see her lounging about his place covered only in one of his big white dress shirts, giving him access to all the curves of her body. The image excited him almost as much as the reality of her before him.

"Maybe later. Do I have to sleep in anything?" She said it with a saucy gleam in her eye.

He still needed to know how they were really going to proceed. Yet, with the beauty of her beckoning him, he put the question from his mind and brought his lips to her shoulder.

In response, she giggled and kicked out her feet in front of her.

He did it again. She giggled again. Another sensitive spot.

When they had been together in college, he had never really taken the time to explore her body like he was doing now. He was learning her secret places for the first time, and he liked being the one who really knew her that way.

He brought his lips back to her shoulder and felt her body tense for another tickle, but instead of kissing it with his lips, he drew his tongue lightly over the spot that made her giggle. Her chest arched forward, and a shiver ran through her body.

He did it again. She brought her arms around him and pressed her lips to his ear and murmured, sending goose bumps down his back and heat into his groin.

He lifted her from the couch, careful not to tear the organza mesh over the skirt of her dress. She wrapped her arms about him and let him carry her into the bedroom. This time, there were no errands to run, no locations to see, no places they had to rush off to.

He pulled down the spread and top sheet and laid her in the middle of his bed. Then he kicked off his shoes and climbed in next to her where he could continue to play with her shoulders.

As he ran his tongue along her shoulder, he smoothed his fingers over the crinkled fabric covering her chest, making her arch toward him. In response, she moved her hand over the front of his pants, teasing him mercilessly.

But he was going to get back at her. He slipped his hand under the wide skirt of her dress and ran it up along her thighs until her body convulsed under his touch. His tongue still played over her shoulder. He wanted to taste every inch of her body, and tonight he would take his time.

Nigel was up before the alarm went off at six. He extricated his limbs from around Regina's sleeping body, shut off the alarm, slipped on his briefs and headed into the kitchen to make them breakfast. He woke her up with a tray of eggs, toast, cereal, milk, juice and coffee.

Regina rubbed her eyes and pulled the covers up over her naked body, but he handed her his shirt from the previous night.

She smiled and slipped into it as he settled into bed beside her with the tray.

"What time is it?"

"It's just after six. That gives us time for breakfast before I get you home."

"Okay." She smiled and dug into the eggs.

"So when can I call you?"

He could no longer avoid the questions of the previous day. He had to know how to proceed from there.

She looked at him. "What?"

"You said I call too much, and I don't want to cramp you. When can I call?"

"I don't know," she said, pouring milk into both of their cereal bowls. "Play it by ear."

"Reggie, our ears are different on this. I was happy with how we were going. You were the one who thought it was getting to be too much."

"It was just starting to seem to get too heavy."

Too much like dating, he thought. The irony wasn't lost on him, them having just been on a real date and all the night before.

"I don't mean to push too hard."

He wasn't saying what he really wanted to say, but he didn't want to chase her away.

"I know," she said. "Eat your cereal before it gets soft."

They ate quietly for a little while.

"I just enjoy spending time with you," he said. "I don't—"

"I do, too. Let's just leave it at that."

He nodded his head. She had shut him down again. There was no way around the blockade. He settled back on the bed, and they turned to their breakfast again. But he had questions that needed to be answered.

When they finished, he put the tray on his nightstand and drew her under his arm.

"I just need to know how to go on from here. I don't

want you avoiding my calls because you think it's getting too heavy."

"Look, Nigel. We're not going to agree on this. Let's let it go and just…"

"Just what? I can't even play it by ear if I don't know what you're thinking."

"I'm thinking that I just want to be friends, enjoy time with you, without it getting too serious."

"Define *too serious*."

"Look," she said. She was agitated and rustled under his arm. "I just can't go back there."

"What about us now? What about me now?"

"I like now, just as it is."

He lifted the arm he had around her to play with the strands of hair that had fallen to her temples.

"Okay, but tell me this. What's so wrong with getting a little serious? The times we've been intimate, didn't you feel anything?"

She backed away from him, clearly flustered. "I just enjoyed it, that's all."

"You seemed to feel something for me last night."

"Nigel, stop pushing for something that's not there."

He was pushing, and he knew he should stop, but something in him wanted her to admit that she had feelings for him, that it was more than physical. They had both gotten to their feet. She had snatched up her things and was pulling her dress up under the shirt he'd given her to wear.

"Wasn't last night real? Didn't you want me? Not sex in general, but me."

"It was what it was. Remember? Nothing more."

He could tell that she was getting more agitated and was ready to go, and he was just as upset. He pulled on his socks and pants and took his shirt from the bed where she'd tossed it. He put it on so that he would be ready to drive her home. No use suggesting a shower together now.

"Are you ready to go?" he asked.

"Yes, but wait." She seemed to have calmed down slightly. She came and sat on the bed next to him and looked at him. "If you're going to get serious, then maybe we should call this off."

He looked at her; she was serious. It made him angry that she could suggest tossing everything aside so easily, as if it didn't really mean anything to her, especially after the night they'd spent together.

"If that's how you see it."

As he said it, matching her nonchalance, he wondered what he was doing. But it was out. And if she could dismiss him so easily, maybe it was for the best.

"Okay," she said and walked into the living room.

Okay, if that's the way she wanted it.

He drove her home in silence and watched her trek up to the third-story landing and go inside. Then he headed back to his place to shower and get to work.

His world had been turned upside down overnight by Regina Gibson. Once she had ended their relationship because he wasn't serious enough. Now she was ending their relationship because he was too serious.

"If you're going to get serious, then maybe we should call this off."

So be it. She wanted a break. She would have a break.

Chapter 17

Regina pulled up the bottom of her overalls and squatted in front of one of her pieces in the spare bedroom that she used as a studio. She'd already carried the bulk of them over to the gallery, leaving anything that had a flaw or that hadn't come out quite right. These she was double-checking. It was her last chance to get things there before the showing, and she wanted as much of her work on display as possible.

She hadn't seen or heard from Nigel in several weeks, and her mind went to him now because he'd been in this room with her. It was here that he'd touched her that time, driving her crazy. She missed having his arms around her, his fingers touching her. She missed knowing that they would be together again.

She'd gotten used to him. That was the problem. Maybe she shouldn't have said they should call it off, but it was the wise thing to do. Between her getting used to him and him turning serious on her, things had gotten muddled beyond clarification.

She turned a tiled sculpture around on the table. Why hadn't she taken this one? The grout color hadn't turned out as she'd wanted it, but she couldn't find anything else wrong, so it went on the table near the door. She'd get one more load of pieces to carry to the gallery tonight, and that would be it. She'd be there late setting up for tomorrow evening.

She'd thought about inviting him to her gallery showing, but that wouldn't make sense. She didn't know if he would even agree to come after she'd called it quits. If he did, that would just start things up again. It would open the door to the same unanswerable questions. Can't we just be friends? Isn't there more going on here?

She lifted a large board to the table and turned the light toward it. What was wrong with this piece? Ah, the grout had pulled away from the tile in one area. It would have to stay.

It didn't make sense thinking about him. She had been the one to call it off. She should just stick to what she'd said and remember why she'd said it: she wasn't going back there.

She got the car loaded, grabbed a sandwich and headed to the Spring View Art Gallery in Silver Spring. Her work would be there for a month, and she hoped that there would be enough sales to boost her depleted savings account. She was putting several ads in the *Washington Post* and had fliers made up to hand out. It was an extra effort, but she needed it to pay off.

She got finished setting up in time to get home, sleep for a few hours and get to work. After that, she came back to change into something suitable for that night. She decided on the gown she'd worn two summers before to a girlfriend's wedding—the turquoise satin one with spaghetti straps that was cut close to her body and that had a matching bolero jacket made out of lace. She finished the outfit with black pumps and a black pocketbook. It was an important night, and she wanted to dress for the occasion.

Once she arrived at the gallery, she saw that most of the people there were people she knew, with a few gallery-goers mixed into the gathering. Then she saw Nigel. He was with Lillith, the manager of the gallery, who was putting a sold sticker on a piece that he was pointing to.

Lillith saw her looking and beckoned her over. "Regina, we've sold our first three pieces—three of the larger ones. This is—"

"Nigel Johns. I know him."

Lillith must have caught the look that passed between them because she excused herself. "Let me go see if I can help some of our other patrons while you catch up. Thank you, Mr. Johns. You can pick these up after the showing. Here's my card."

As she passed by Regina, she pointed discreetly at Nigel, mouthed "hottie" and gave Regina a wink. Lillith was such a prim matron that the gestures made Regina laugh.

Once Lillith was gone, Regina found herself smiling up at Nigel. She couldn't help feeling glad to see him.

"Hello, Nigel. I'm surprised to see you here. I thought about giving you a call to let you know about the show, but then, we weren't really…in touch."

"I found out from Amelie and saw one of your announcements in the *Post*."

"Did Amelie get you her info for the application?"

"Not yet, but she's been in contact to let me know that she's pulling it together."

"Oh, good," Regina said. "We're going out this week together to look at more locations."

"Let me know how it goes. I think that's all you need now."

"I know."

He backed up to point at one of the mosaics he'd purchased.

"I came early to get the pick of the litter. I'm sending a few of my clients along to take a look as well, and one's a new restaurant owner. I had to get mine before they came in and took the best ones. This is one of the ones I'm getting."

"Nigel, you don't have to buy anything. Just coming out to show your support is more than enough."

"No, I actually needed at least three pieces—one to add color to the living room, one for the bedroom and one to show off in my office."

"You didn't have to get them here. You got large ones, and these are gallery prices. I could have—"

"It's worth paying them, especially when one day I'll own the work of a famous artist."

Regina couldn't help smiling.

"Thank you. Now let me tell you how to take care of them."

"How about over a late supper? What time do you get through here?"

"We close at eight tonight, but I don't know if it's a good idea for us to…get together."

"I've missed you terribly, Reggie. Come to dinner with me."

Before she could answer, he stepped toward her, pulled her into his arms and bent down to claim her lips. His kiss was so sudden, so passionate, that it knocked the breath out of her and started a throbbing in her center. He pulled away just as quickly.

"I won't take no as an answer."

When they stepped apart, she glanced around in time to see Jason giving her a naughty look. She laughed out loud. Being with this man made her act silly.

Nigel looked over and saw Jason and nodded to him and Ellison before waving to Kyle, who waved back from his place on Ellison's hip. He struggled to get down, and when Ellison relented, he ran over to Nigel.

Nigel picked him up and gave him a hug.

"Here, give Auntie Regina a kiss."

Nigel held Kyle like an airplane and the little one giggled as he landed on Regina and gave her a kiss.

"Okay," said Nigel. "That's enough. Those lips are spoken for."

Regina raised her finger to protest but thought the better of it. There was such a simple pleasure in the moment that she didn't want to spoil it.

"Were you going out with friends after to celebrate the opening?"

"A few of us were going to go to dinner. You can join us if you'd like."

"That would be nice.

"And can I see you after dinner, as well?"

"I'm not sure we should…hang out."

"There's no getting out of it, Reggie. I've missed you too much."

Kyle started struggling to get down. Nigel put him on his feet, and they watched him until he'd returned to his parents, who were talking with Amelie now.

Nigel pulled Regina into his arms again.

"Haven't you missed me, too?"

"Well...I guess." She was trying to deny it but couldn't. They both broke out laughing.

"If you don't admit it, I'll have to use unorthodox means to get you to confess."

He turned his fingers into spiders and ran them up her stomach. She giggled and tried to shoo him away.

"Okay, yes."

"I'm sorry," he said. "I'm just in a funny mood tonight. It's seeing you and seeing that you're glad to see me."

Lillith came up to them.

"We have another purchase. Come meet the buyers."

"Clients of yours?" she asked Nigel.

"No, they're not." He kissed her temple. "I'll go say hello to your friends while you go do your thing."

He walked over to her group of friends standing next to the wine and cheese table, and she gave her attention to Lillith and the customers. After that, Lillith drew her around the exhibit to talk to visitors. It was delightful to hear their comments on her work and to answer questions. Not many were buying, but she hoped that at least a few would come back another time.

Whenever she glanced over, she found Nigel talking to Jason, Ellison and Amelie. From the looks of it, they were having a good time together; they all seemed jovial.

When it was almost eight, she turned from the guest she'd been talking to and found Lillith, who was writing a receipt out for the last purchase of the night.

"We sold over a dozen pieces. For a relatively unknown artist, that's great. It bodes well for the rest of the show. We also had a great turnout."

"Well, I had a lot of my friends come in tonight."

"Keep them coming."

"I will. I made cards to send out to everyone I know and everyone I've ever worked with and everyone I've ever taken classes from. If there are any left over, I'll hand them out to strangers on the street."

"That's great. Wait. Let me dim the lights so people know it's time to go."

Lillith dimmed the lights and then brought them all the way up. The remaining guests started meandering toward the door, so Regina went to say good-night and hand out her business cards to them as they left. It was just after eight when she sought out the little group that had been waiting for her.

"We're going to have to cut out," said Jason.

"No, but you waited all this time," she responded.

"I know, but this one's getting tired. He's been getting a bit antsy."

She pursed her lips and fingered Kyle's little tummy. "Is the little one tired?"

"We're gonna stop for some fast food and get him home."

"Okay." She hugged Kyle, then Ellison, then Jason. "Thank you so much for coming tonight."

"I'm going, too," said Amelie. "I have to be at Eastern Market tomorrow morning for setup."

She hugged Amelie. "Everybody's going?"

"Not me," said Nigel, coming to place a hand on her back.

"Did you do this? Did you chase my friends away?"

He raised his hands in innocence.

"Don't look at me. Eight o'clock on a Friday. Folks are tired."

She smacked his shoulder playfully, not fully believing his story.

Lillith came out and started wrapping up the cheese and crackers.

"Can I stay to do anything?" asked Regina.

"Nope. You've done your part. Head home. I'll see you next week."

"Okay," she said and hugged Lillith. "Thank you for everything."

"Good night, Regina. Good night, Mr. Johns."

They waved and headed to their cars.

Nigel pressed his palm on the small of Regina's back as they walked to her car. She was radiant in her shimmering gown, and it fit her body in a way that teased him with her every curve. It was her special night, and she looked it.

But it was his night, too. His reentry into her life had gone much better than he had dared to hope. He had been ready to dispute, debate and rebut, but he didn't have to. The bond between them had just been there.

As beautiful as she looked tonight, he just wanted to take her out so that the world could see that she was with him. And as sexy as she looked tonight, he just wanted to take her home where she would be only his.

"How do we do this?" she asked. "Should I follow you? Where are we going?"

"We're in Silver Spring. Let's go park in the lot for the mall. They have restaurants over there."

"Okay. We'll meet there."

They stayed close to one another on the road and parked next to each other in the lot.

They decided on Italian food and entered the restaurant together.

Over dinner, he kept smiling at her. She couldn't help smiling back.

"What?" she asked.

"You missed me."

She swatted at him across the table, but he knew that she couldn't rightly deny it. After this, they both knew that she was going home with him to make love. It wasn't because he insisted; it was because she wanted him, too, even if she wouldn't say it out loud.

"And you love me," he added.

She raised her hand, and he could tell that she was about to tell him a thing or two about the assumptions he was making, but he cut in.

"Don't get all in a huff." He smiled at her. "It's okay if you don't know it yet. And it's okay if you want to pretend it's not serious. I won't rush you."

"Your smug, know-it-all attitude is starting to piss me off," she said, but she couldn't hold her angry tone and broke out in a smile. "I'll correct you later. Right now, let's enjoy our food and tonight."

He touched her arm. "Tonight." He looked into her eyes, and the passion he saw there made him take a breath.

"I want you, Reggie."

He took her hand.

"Let's finish eating first," she said. She took a deep breath, and he could tell she was trying not to give herself away.

He smiled. "Okay. So how did the show go?"

"It went well. We sold over a dozen pieces."

"Congratulations, honey."

The rest of dinner was light conversation. Then they followed each other to his apartment.

They started kissing before the elevator door closed, and by the time they reached his floor, they were wrapped in each other's arms. Nigel closed the door to his apartment and pressed her against it with his body. Regina could feel the full length of him.

One of his hands came between them to cup her breast, and the other traveled up her thigh to grip her buttocks.

She murmured against his lips, and in response, he parted her lips, and his low groan filled her mouth.

She felt one of his legs come between hers and spread her thighs apart, and she opened for him, feeling his fingers begin to explore her through her clothes. She began to throb as his knuckles gently grazed the front of her gown, finding her center and sending tingles spreading throughout her body.

She lifted herself onto her toes to try to feel more of him, and he lifted her from her feet against his body, her back pressed to the door. Heat filled her center as it pressed onto his, and she couldn't help the moan that filled her throat and passed into his mouth.

He let her down and drew her to the bedroom.

She took off his suit jacket and hung it on the back of his chair. He unzipped her gown and sat on the edge of his bed, drawing her between his knees so that he could run his mouth over the fabric of her bra, licking her nipples into hard peaks while she gasped for air. When he ran his hand between her thighs and began to knead the wet slip of her panties, she bucked against his fingers and moaned.

Regina wanted to play, as well. She pushed Nigel back onto the bed, unbuttoned his shirt and brought her lips to one of his nipples. Her soft bites made him writhe, but not enough, so she ran her hand along the front of his pants until his body was jerking with her every touch and his groan filled her ears.

They stood to remove the rest of their clothes, and Nigel dug in his dresser for a condom. She took it from him. She sat on the edge of his bed and pulled him before her. She ran her hand over the hard ripples of his chest and down the firm line of his belly before opening the packet and taking out the slick disc. Then she rolled it onto him, and her mouth followed the path it had taken.

He moaned and called her name, spreading his fingers into her hair. When he stepped back from her, his eyes were glazed with passion, and he exhaled deeply. He moved onto the bed, covering her body.

"I want you, Reggie."

"I want you, too, Nigel."

She clung to his shoulders as he moved inside of her, finding her mouth again and filling her with his heat and his presence. He began to thrust against her, making her womanhood throb as his chest dragged along her breasts.

Then he found the place that made her lunge against him, and his long prods became short thrusts, making her cry out and gasp, making pressure begin to build in her center because he was pushing her toward the edge.

"Do you love me, Reggie?" he asked.

She heard him as from afar.

"Do you love me, Reggie?"

At first she couldn't answer; the pleasure mounting inside her blocked out rational thought, comprehensible language.

"Do you love me?"

Her body clenched.

"Yes."

"Do you love me?"

She felt the first wave of her explosion moving through her.

She cried out. "Yes."

"Do you love me?"

She moved along him as she was pushed over the edge.

"Yes, Nigel, yes."

Her sex began to quiver, and she pressed it against his length.

"Yes, yes."

* * *

Nigel felt Regina's body grip his even tighter. Her hands pressed into his back. Her hips tilted upward to meet his. Her thrusts matched his.

"Yes, Nigel."

Her answer was music to his ears, driving him toward the precipice. And once her voice was unleashed, she couldn't seem to stop it; it had become a mantra.

"Yes," she said and cried out.

Her legs began to shake at his hips, and her breath became short and labored.

"I do. I need you. Please."

He felt her body grip on to his again.

"Please what? I'll do anything."

"Don't stop."

"I won't."

Her womanhood clamped around him, causing him to buck. He felt the waves of her contraction as it pulsed through her and along his manhood.

"Yes," she called out, "yes."

Nigel could only groan as he plunged within her, driven over the edge.

They lay together as their breathing slowed. A broad smile spread across Nigel's face. She had said yes.

As their bodies cooled, she turned in his arms and raised herself on her elbows to see his face, which wore a silly grin.

"I knew you did," he said.

She slapped his arm. "No. I can't be held accountable for what I say in the throes of lovemaking."

"When you're not censoring yourself?"

"When I'm not thinking at all."

"I don't believe you. Or rather, I do."

She ran her hand down his face to try to get rid of his satisfied grin. "Stop smiling like that. I didn't know what I was saying."

She settled back down next to him, concern filling her. Soon they would start to make love again. Only, this time, it was making love and not just having sex. She was in love again—in love with Nigel Johns.

Chapter 18

Nigel picked his way through the crowd inside Eastern Market. The meat looked plump and fresh. If he wasn't hoping to get Regina to go to a movie with him, he would get some lamb shanks and some pork chops. In fact, as good as they looked, he still might.

He'd never been to Eastern Market before, much less on a cool weekend day near the end of summer. The place was packed. Inside, the shoppers filled the central aisle and formed packed lines in front of every counter. They were two or three deep in front of the produce bins, and as fresh as it looked, Nigel could understand why. He'd gotten some peaches from one of the farmers out front under the outdoor tent.

"Excuse me." He stopped an older woman. "Where would I find the jewelry and art?"

"That's at the flea market outside. Go through that door over there, and you'll see the booths."

"Thank you, ma'am."

"You're welcome."

He followed her directions to an area outside that was bigger than the indoor food market and separate from the farmer's market out front. Here, he started making his way through aisles of booths that had just about anything you could name. Furniture, crafts, housewares, art, jewelry, clothes, books, imports—more than he could have imagined.

He saw Amelie's jewelry first.

"Hey," she said as they hugged. "What are you doing here?"

"I'm looking for your partner."

"She just went to get us some drinks. She'll be back in a minute. Let me just help this lady, and then we can chat."

Amelie turned back to her customer, and he turned around to find some of Regina's mosaics on the opposite side of the table. They were mostly smaller pieces, ones that could be moved more easily. They were piled and stacked, with some out front as accents. This setting didn't allow them to be displayed properly.

The booth in front of them was an importer of African clothing—the kind Amelie and Regina wore often. Now he knew where they got them. Next to them was a glass-worker's booth with everything from vases to plates. On the other side were exotic wooden pieces, some furniture but mostly light fixtures and ornaments. Behind them was a textile booth; he wasn't sure what was being sold there, perhaps tablecloths or wall hangings, maybe just material. Every direction had something unique.

"Can I help you?"

He turned around to find that it was Regina. She handed a bottle of juice to Amelie and turned back to him.

"Nigel, I didn't recognize you from behind without a suit on."

He stepped back and turned around with his arms out. He had on a white T-shirt, a blue sweat suit, striped sneakers and a baseball cap. He was showing her that he could do casual.

She smiled at him, but only for a moment. She wasn't as cheerful today.

"Actually, you *can* help me," he said. "I need something smallish that I can send to my mom. Her birthday's coming up. I was thinking about one of your mosaic African sculptures."

"Mosaics are heavy. It's pricey to mail them."

She didn't have many sculptures out, but he saw one that was what he had in mind. "How about this piece?"

"Why not some perfume? A nice dress?"

"Is she trying to talk you out of a sale, Nigel?" asked Amelie, smiling.

"Yes, she is."

"He's done too much already, Amelie. He got three pieces at the gallery—larger ones. That's more than enough."

Luckily, Amelie paid her no mind.

"Which one do you like, Nigel?"

"I was thinking about this one for my mom."

"Oh, I like that one, too."

Amelie picked it up and looked at the bottom. "It's $185, but for you, we can do $150. How's that?"

"I'll do the $185. Do you take checks?"

"From you we do. Make it out to Beads and Tiles."

"I like your new name better."

Amelie doubled a shopping bag, wrapped the sculpture in newspaper and placed it carefully into the bottom of the bag. "So do I. We think African-American Beadwork and Mosaic Arts works better for us now. I'm sorry we don't have a gift box, but if you go to The Wrap Store, you'll find something."

Regina had been quiet while he made the purchase. Now she turned to Amelie. "Do you mind if I steal Nigel away for a few minutes? I need to talk to him. Can I walk you to your car?"

"No, I'm still looking for another present for my mom, and this is my first time around the market. Walk around with me. Here." He handed Amelie the bag of peaches. "These can be for you guys."

He hugged Regina when she stepped around the booth and tugged her toward the booths he hadn't seen yet.

She went along with him without saying anything, not even when he pointed out an African dress that his mom might like. He tugged her hand.

"Hey, what's wrong?"

"Nigel, I can't see you anymore."

"What? Why?"

"I can't say. I can only say that I can't see you anymore."

"Not again. We just went through this. I told you, I won't rush you. If you just want to call us friends, that's fine. Whatever you want."

She pulled her hand out of his.

"It's not any of that. I just can't see you anymore—for good this time."

"Why?"

She looked around. They were between two booths, and other shoppers were skirting around them. He could see her distraction.

"This is not the best place to talk," he said. "What time are you through tonight?"

"There isn't anything to talk about. I just can't continue to see you."

Her eyes were misty. He could tell that she was serious this time, but he wasn't about to let her go—not without a real reason and not without a fight.

"What time do you close down?"

She sighed. "We shut down at six. I'm home by seven."

"Do you need help breaking things down?"

"No, no. But—"

"I'll be at your place waiting."

He walked her back to the booth and hugged Amelie.

He had several hours. He had thought that today he would be doing some window-shopping and getting movie tickets, maybe helping them break things down at the booth.

Instead, he was again fretting over the newest incarnation of Regina Gibson—the newest ultimatum.

He doubled back to the indoor market, stopping to get some more peaches on the way in. He went inside and got some lamb shanks and pork chops, some pasta and sauce, some bread and some fresh flowers.

He got home, cooked the lamb shanks and the pasta, showered and changed. He still had time to kill before going to wait for Regina, so while he packed up the meal to take with him, he called his mother to ask her what she wanted for her birthday.

"Oh, honey, I don't need a thing."

He knew she would say that. She always did. Regina's suggestion of perfume wasn't a bad idea, and maybe an African dress to round it out. He would get an extra box from the department store for the statue and put everything in one large box to mail.

He talked to his mom for a little bit, just finding out how things were at home. It helped to calm him down when he was riled up, even if she didn't know there was anything going on with him.

He got to Regina's apartment early, toted dinner up to the third floor landing and waited for her on the bottom step. It wasn't too long before she came home, and he got up to meet her at her car.

"Can I help you unload things?"

"No, everything for Eastern Market stays in Amelie's car. Look, Nigel, I don't think there's anything to talk about."

"Yes, Reggie, there is."

He followed her up the steps, where she found the bag he'd placed at her door.

"That's dinner, but these are for you."

He took out the bouquet he'd gotten from the market— Birds of Paradise and other exotic long-stemmed flowers. They drew her in for a second look.

"They're beautiful. Thank you. But—"

"They don't change your mind. I know. That's not why I got them."

She was clearly hesitant about letting them into her apartment, but she did.

"Are you hungry now, or should we talk first?"

She didn't seem to want to do either, so he nudged. "Why don't we eat now, while the food is warm and the wine is cold? Then we can talk without rushing."

She rolled her eyes but pointed to the cabinet for him to get out plates. Reluctantly, she followed suit and took out the silverware, napkins, two water glasses and two wineglasses. She pulled two place mats from the corner of the table and set places for them.

"I hope it turned out all right. I don't make lamb shanks often."

"That sounds fancy."

"No, my parents made them at home every now and then. I got six at Eastern Market, so dig in."

"This is a lot of food. I think one will be enough for me."

"Not if you don't fill up on pasta," he said and chuckled.

"Nigel, we're just delaying the inevitable."

"Just until after dinner. Let's catch up on other things for a while."

He passed her the bread, and they began eating. Over dinner they talked about everything that wasn't the real issue at hand: how her father was doing, how the search for a new location was going, how her art show was doing, how his work was going, what he invested in, how his cousin Michelle was doing.

They seemed like a regular couple, but they both knew that the difficult part was still coming. While Regina cleared the plates, he refreshed their wineglasses. She came back to the table and sat across from him.

"If I'd known we were eating in, I'd have gotten dessert," she said.

"I'm stuffed, no dessert for me."

"Me, too. Thank you for dinner."

Nigel leaned over the table and took Regina's hand. He exhaled slowly and launched in.

"You don't want to see me anymore."

"No."

He waited for more.

She shook her head. "I just don't think we should continue. I can't continue. It's been… I've enjoyed our time. I just can't let it go on."

"Why? What's changed?"

"I've been ambivalent about this all along. But it keeps getting muddled."

"What's changed in the last week?"

"I—"

She started, but she stopped. He could tell that there

was something that she wasn't telling him, something that he needed to know.

"Tell me."

"I can't say. Just take my word for it."

"If you expect me to stay away from you, I need to know why."

She turned to him with tears in her eyes. "Because I think I'm in love with you. I can't—"

Nigel whooped out loud, broke out in a grin, lifted her from her chair and spun her around. He let her down against his chest, caressing her loose hair.

"It's about time you figured that out."

He laughed, rubbing her back. It was a weight lifted off him, a weight lifted off the evening. He couldn't stop smiling.

She put her hand up to his chest, shaking her head. It was then that he realized she was crying.

"Reggie, what's wrong? This is great. I love you so much."

He wrapped his arm around her and stroked her back until she broke free.

"No, stop. I can't do this."

"You love me. I love you. Where's the problem?"

He was mystified. He needed her to make sense of this for him. She went into the living room, and he followed. She paced a few times and then turned to him.

"I look at you, and sometimes I remember the baby I lost. I remember the nights I cried my eyes out because my marriage never happened. I remember…"

It made sense to him now, but he couldn't accept it. He wouldn't accept it as the end of their relationship.

"Why not just see me? See where we are now. See who I am now. It's not about going back there. It's about being here."

He sat on her sofa and pulled her down with him onto his lap.

"I love you. I can't change the past, but I can make us a present and a future."

He kissed the tracks of her tears, and then he took her lips with his. He kissed her until she was kissing him back.

"It's always been that way with us," he said.

"I just don't know. I don't know if I can do it…again."

"Let's just see where it goes."

He kissed her again, and she curled against his chest.

"Is it okay if we just see where it goes with us being in love?"

Her head was against his neck, and he felt her move slightly. She was nodding.

Chapter 19

Regina shifted under Nigel's arm and put her head on his shoulder.

It had been a couple of months since she had given in to her feelings for Nigel, since they had started really seeing one another, but it still felt new to her.

"If I'm supposed to be giving directions, why am I in the backseat?" asked Jason.

The group laughed.

"Because you wanted to sit next to your love thing," Amelie replied. "Here, give me the directions."

"Oh, no," Regina said. "Amelie got us lost going to Prince George's Plaza."

The group laughed again.

"How is the little one?" Nigel asked.

Ellison looked at Kyle, who was in the backseat with them in a child safety seat.

"After all the food and rides today at the amusement

park, he's out like a light again. We'll have to wake him for dinner."

They'd rented a minivan for the drive back from Ocean City, where they'd spent the Labor Day weekend. Jason, Ellison and Kyle were in the third row; Amelie was stretched out by herself in the middle; and Regina was up front with Nigel, who was behind the wheel.

They'd driven up on Thursday afternoon and walked the boardwalk that evening. Friday and Saturday they'd hit the beach and done some shopping—at least Regina and Amelie had. Kyle had gone with them, and the men had played miniature golf. Both nights they had gone to the movies and to dinner.

Sunday they had slept in, hit the beach and gone to a nightclub (except for Amelie, who stayed to watch Kyle). Monday was the amusement park, and it was all about little Kyle. They were driving back late that afternoon, early enough to get rested for work the next day.

Regina's body was still vibrating from all of the love she and Nigel had made. Even after last night, they still stole an hour to be with each other again when they were supposed to be packing to leave. Everyone was waiting for them in the lobby and teased them when they got down.

They stopped for lunch halfway to DC and finished the last leg of the three-hour drive in one straight shot.

"Hey, whose idea was this trip?" Ellison asked.

"Nigel's," Regina said.

"Props. It was a blast. We have to do it again."

"I'm in," Amelie said.

"Me, too," Regina echoed.

"Hey, put on some of that old school you had on during the drive up."

Nigel plugged his MP3 player in, and the guys started talking about the song, singing with it and telling its history. Regina started to pull away because Nigel's body had become animated, bouncing her head, but he pulled her back and settled down a bit.

"Sorry." He glanced over his shoulder. "Did we wake Kyle?"

"Nope," Jason said, "he yawned and kept on sleeping."

The group laughed.

"I think I need some sleep, as well," Regina said.

"I know why," Amelie said. "Something's keeping you up nights."

"Hush," Regina said.

"Too late," Ellison said. "I heard it, and I concur."

Regina turned into Nigel's shoulder for a moment. Nigel, perhaps to save her further embarrassment, steered the conversation elsewhere.

"You know, it's a good thing we're in DC already so I don't actually need directions."

Everyone laughed again.

"I told you," Jason said. "I shouldn't be in the back."

"Look," Amelie said. "It's our old place. It's all changed. Can we stop and look?"

Regina lifted her head to see. Her spirits fell at the same time.

"What kind of business is it now, a restaurant?" she asked.

The structure itself was different. The building had been entirely redone. There was a larger first floor with wide windows and a raised ceiling, and there were two regular stories on top.

"Yeah, let's stop," Jason said.

"You okay with this?" Nigel asked her.

"Sure."

Looking at the old place without a new one in sight

brought her down, but she didn't want to spoil it for the others.

They parked out back and walked around to the front, Nigel leading the way.

"Hey, it's open," he said.

"Let's go inside," Amelie said.

Inside, Jason found the lights.

Regina looked about, feeling like a thief. Then she got confused. Along one wall was a station that would be perfect for beads: a counter of inset bowls, a wall of pegs for strings of beads. The front was set up for displays.

Regina took another step inside and stopped. A long display case in the middle of the room was already stocked. Regina's eyes flew open. She recognized Amelie's jewelry right away, and next to those pieces were her own mosaics—pieces that Amelie was supposed to have in storage for their booth at Eastern Market.

Regina's head was spinning as she tried to make sense of it all. These were her things. Somehow, they'd gotten back the space. Somehow her dream for this place, for her art, had come true. Her heart was filling up with hope. It was too good to be real. Had they really gotten the space? How?

"What have you done, Nigel?"

Amelie linked arms with her and pulled her farther inside, almost squealing. "Come look."

"You're in on this, too?"

Amelie couldn't stop talking. "Look, there are windows for display cases big enough to be spotted from the street, brand-new counters and workstations, two large classrooms."

"What have you guys done?"

"Look." Amelie pulled her toward the back. "There's even a small separate room for your ceramic kilns and my pewter kiln. There are boxes of supplies piled in the class-rooms. All you have to do is say yes."

"Look at your new sign," Jason said.

She gave him a look. "Why would all of you gang up on me?"

Ellison held a still-sleeping Kyle on his shoulder. "Consider it an intervention, honey," he said. "Go with the flow."

She turned toward the front of the store and read the huge sign that hadn't yet been hung out front—African-American Beadwork and Mosaic Arts.

Tears came to her eyes.

She turned to Amelie. "Our paperwork isn't even in yet. Even with full drafts, we still need…"

"A location. Here it is."

"You'd been procrastinating so long getting the info to Nigel that I was worried that you might be thinking of backing out."

"Back out nothing! We found a private lender, honey. Look at it. There's even an extra floor upstairs; you can have a real home now. Or we can rent it out."

"I bet I know who the private lender is."

She turned to Nigel.

"I said that I wanted to help. I've wanted to tell you so many times so that you'd stop worrying about finding another location."

"We made sure we were with you in case we needed to talk you out of a good place," Amelie said, "but one never materialized."

"How did this happen?"

Nigel stepped toward her and put his arm around her shoulder.

"We were able to get it back from the person Mr. Lundstrum sold it to before any remodeling was done. Then we got an architect who could get all the paperwork done and redo the place the way you wanted it."

"I told him what we talked about and helped with the plans," Amelie said. "The whole place had to be demolished. I hope we got it right, Regina. We couldn't ask you exactly what you wanted."

"Why didn't you tell me?"

"We couldn't," Amelie said.

"Every time I tried to bring it up, you got defensive, Reggie. In the end, I thought I should just pursue it on my own. At worst, it would be an improved property to put back on the market, and you'd hate me for trying. But at best, you'd have a good location that you can afford in the condition that you need it to be in."

Nigel was still trying to gauge her reaction. Amelie was almost giddy. Jason and Ellison were hanging back, looking around. She was still trying to take it all in and get her bearings so that she knew what her reaction should be.

"It's beautiful. But I don't know if I want to owe you money, Nigel."

"It's him or the banks, honey," Amelie said. "Guess which one is more likely to pull a fast one. Actually, it's him *and* the banks." She turned to Nigel. "Can I tell her?"

"Tell me what?"

"Our paperwork is in to the bank. It went in a long time ago, and we have an angel investor." Regina caught Nigel giving Amelie the head-chopping signal about the last part; Amelie wasn't supposed to have said that.

"I know what an angel investor is," Regina said.

"What is it?" Ellison asked.

"It's someone who provides capital for a business just starting out," Jason answered, "or who agrees to pay on a loan if you default."

"Look, we have an agreement from National Bank,"

Amelie said. "That's not even included in this." She opened her arms to indicate the location.

"Reggie," Nigel said, "new companies are less likely to fail if they have angel investors."

"You can use it for advertising," Ellison said.

"And if you sign these," Nigel said, taking papers out of the cash register, "you won't be a renter here, you'll be the *owner*. The bank loan has to be paid on once you sign for it, but you'll have as much time as you want to make good on this place. No strings attached—to anything."

"Please, Regina," Amelie said. "We have our dream back. We're not going to find another location like this that we can afford."

She walked around and ended up in front of Jason. He drew her in for a hug, and then she stepped back to look up at him.

"It's up to you, kiddo," he said, "but it's a good opportunity."

She went back to Amelie and Nigel.

"It's just what we wanted," she said to Amelie. She looked at Amelie and then at Nigel. "I'll do it."

Amelie squealed and hugged her, and they started bouncing up and down, and soon both of them were crying. Linked arm in arm, they started circling the room again, seeing what it was now that it was theirs.

In the end, she stood before Nigel.

"Nigel, could you really afford to do all this? Didn't it empty your bank account?"

"Yes, I could, and no, it didn't."

"Thank you so much, Nigel. I'll pay you back every penny."

"It was my pleasure, Reggie."

She put her arms around him and hugged him. In response, he dipped his head down and kissed her.

"I just want to see you happy, Reggie. And I want your talent to get recognized."

"I can't thank you enough."

"You don't have to thank me. Just get to work," he said and chuckled.

Gratitude filled Regina's heart and filled her eyes with tears. Nigel was kidding, but what he had done—this gift—would change her life. She didn't know what to say. She reached up to his cheek and ran her fingers along its curve while tears ran down her face. He took her hand and put her fingers to his lips then pulled her into an embrace.

She looked up at him, and he leaned down and kissed her again, first soft then strong. Their lips spelled out the tenderness that had grown between them.

"Ahem," said Ellison. "Shall we see the apartment upstairs?"

Everyone else laughed, and they broke the kiss.

"Yes," Nigel said, "let's."

They locked up downstairs and headed out back, where Ellison handed Kyle to Jason for the climb upstairs. The apartment was fully new and partially furnished. Now it opened into the living room with the kitchen off to the left.

There were brand-new appliances, a dinette set, a sectional sofa and matching end tables, an entertainment center. It was all clean and empty.

Regina tapped Nigel on the arm. "You had your designer pick stuff out, didn't you?"

He chuckled. "No, Amelie and I did this all on our own."

"There's a small bedroom on this floor," Amelie said, "but the master bedroom, master bath and studio space are upstairs. Come see."

"I'll wait here," Nigel said. "I have this thing about seeing Reggie in bedrooms."

Regina blushed as the group broke out laughing.

"Here," Nigel said, "I'll hold Kyle."

Jason handed the little one over.

Amelie led the group upstairs. There was a four-poster in the master suite, with a dresser and nightstand. There were two walk-in closets and a huge bath. The studio space had its own small bathroom, as well.

Regina led them back down and took a seat next to Nigel on the sofa.

"When did you start all this? How did you get it done so quickly?"

"I started looking into it the day you came to my office thinking that I was the one who'd purchased the place."

"And our paperwork went to the bank the day after I ditched you two for our meeting."

"Are you going to move back in here?" Ellison asked.

"I don't know. I feel like I just moved. Would it be better to rent it out and put that down as business income? It would be far more than I'm paying."

"It would be your income," Amelie said. "Right?" she asked Nigel.

"Yes, downstairs is equally owned by both of you. Up here we drew up as yours, like a condo. And where you live doesn't matter as long as the business gets off its feet. It's up to you, but yes, while you're still working to establish yourself, it's better to have the income from this place."

"We have to go over all the papers so I'll know what we're doing," Regina said. She turned toward Amelie. "There's so much to talk about."

"We can do that," Nigel said.

"I'm in," Amelie said.

"Is it too early for dinner?" Ellison asked.

The group cracked up.

This time, the laughter woke up Kyle, who was lying

next to Nigel on the sofa. Nigel picked him up and set him into a sitting position.

"We'll let you decide," Nigel said to Kyle. "You hungry?"

The little one thought about it then shook his head yes.

"How about I fill them in another day and we just go to eat?"

"Word," Ellison said.

At the car, Amelie and Regina stopped to do a happy dance and ended up bouncing up and down and yelling.

"That's all the repayment I need," Nigel said to Jason.

Chapter 20

Nigel spooned a second helping of pasta onto their plates while Regina poured more water into their goblets.

"When are you going to come home with me and see my parents again?" Nigel asked. "They haven't seen you in years."

Regina smiled. "That would be nice. I still have friends there."

"So you'll come?" He smiled at her, thinking about holding her on the long ride home.

"Sure. The weekend flea market at Eastern Market ends soon. But the studio opens again in a couple of weeks, and our classes start again not long after that." She was excited about the reopening and about her teaching. "We already have people enrolled in classes for Thursday and Saturday, and we haven't even opened yet. Your advice on advertising has really paid off. Thank you."

"You never have to thank me, Reggie." He pulled her

hand to him and kissed it. "Maybe we should go home after you guys get going. Maybe for Thanksgiving."

"My parents will die if I'm not there for Thanksgiving. You coming?"

"Am I invited?"

She smiled at him. "Yes, but you'll have to stay in the den."

"I can live with that. Okay, a compromise. Take off an extra day for Columbus Day, and we go home to South Carolina. Then we go to New Jersey for Thanksgiving."

"Okay. What about Christmas?" she asked.

"Why don't we do Christmas here together, just the two of us?"

She thought of them wrapped in each other's arms in front of his fireplace with glasses of cider.

"That sounds nice. My parents won't be happy, but hopefully we'll be doing a lot of business, and I'll need to stay anyway. I'm doing a series of mosaic crosses for Christmas. They're easy to do, and they sell well. I'm also making one for my aunt. I can go up for New Year's."

"If we keep it up," he said, "we'll have parceled out every holiday through Easter before dinner is over."

They chuckled.

Regina finished first and folded her napkin. She got up and rounded Nigel's chair and bent over to wrap her arms around his neck. She hummed.

"Finish up."

Nigel cut his pork chop, added a forkful of pasta and brought it to his mouth.

As he took the bite, Regina pressed her lips to his neck, and as he savored the mouthful, she rubbed her hands along his chest, undoing his buttons as she went along.

"What are you doing?"

"Nothing. Go ahead and eat."

By the time Nigel took another mouthful, Regina had his shirt partway down his back. She moved her lips from his neck down to the back of one of his shoulder blades and bit down gently. She ran her tongue over the surface, and then she moved a piece of ice she'd been sucking on between her lips and drew it along the surface.

Nigel's chest heaved outward, and his shoulders flexed backward.

"Finish your dinner, honey," she prodded.

Nigel eyed her over his shoulder and found a mischievous grin on her face. She wanted to play, and he loved when she wanted to play.

As he brought another forkful of pasta to his mouth, Regina pressed her warm tongue to the back of his neck. As he swallowed, she pressed the ice to the spot, feeling his torso straighten.

As he cut another slice of his pork chop, she picked the ice out of her mouth and brought her lips to his ear. She licked the inside of the lobe as she brought the ice to one of his nipples. His chest clenched inward, and he swallowed hard.

"Do you like that?"

"Yes."

"I want proof."

She ran her hand along the crease in his pants, and when she found what she was looking for, his thighs flexed, and he sucked in a breath.

"You're not eating."

"I think I'm finished."

"Aw." Regina straightened up. "I don't want to stop you from finishing your dinner."

As she stepped away, Nigel scooted back his chair and pulled her onto his lap, making her laugh.

"I'm finished. Look." She found his plate nearly empty. "And you don't get away that easily."

His first touch tickled her and set Regina to laughing again. But when his mouth found her neck and his hand found her breast, Regina murmured. He toyed with her body until she twisted on his lap.

"Do you like that?" he asked.

"Yes."

"I want proof."

Nigel slipped his hand under her dress and moved them up her thighs. Regina laughed again, making Nigel laugh. She got up briefly and repositioned herself over his legs, straddling him as she covered his lips with her own.

"Let me feel you," she said, scooting closer to his chest.

He gripped her buttocks and pulled her onto his body. She tilted her hips to meet him and settled along his body. She pulled the straps of her dress from over her shoulders, put her arms around his neck and rubbed her breasts across his chest.

The heat that ran through her body made her murmur against his ear. She licked the lobe of his ear and felt his body tense.

He drew his fingers over her bra, kneading her nipples into peaks. At the same time, he took over her mouth. Regina's body started pulsing, and she rocked along his thighs.

Feeling her oscillate over his manhood drove Nigel to distraction, and he groaned, glaring at her for wreaking such havoc on him. He wanted to make her feel that way also.

"I still want proof," he said, slipping his hand between them and running his fingers over her slick panties.

"You're so wet."

Regina tensed, self-conscious, and started to pull back.

"No, don't go. I love you wet."

He pressed his thumb over her womanhood and began to knead her, and Regina moaned, gripping onto his shoulders.

When Nigel stood, Regina linked her legs around his waist and held on to his neck. He let them down in the middle of his bed, running his body up and down along hers so that she could feel how ready he was to be inside of her. He felt her tilt toward him and pull down on his hips, wanting to feel more. He continued until she moaned and cried out, clinging to him.

When he lifted himself away from her, she grumbled and held on to him.

"Don't stop."

"I'll be right back. I want to be inside of you, baby."

He rifled in his drawer for a condom, removed his clothes and came back to relieve her of the dress that was knotted about her waist and the panties beneath them, as well as her bra and sandals.

She grasped his sheathed member and drew him to her.

"I want you, Nigel."

His body leapt in her hand, and he climbed onto the bed, positioning himself above her. Regina surprised him. She pushed him down instead, and straddled his thighs.

"Is this okay?" she asked once she had him pinned.

He could tell that she was unsure in this position. They had never done this before. "Yes. I love seeing you this way. You look beautiful."

Regina moved her hips, drawing herself over his rigid member and making them both moan. She reached the end and moved back the other way, teasing them both.

Nigel groaned and thrust his hips upward.

"If you keep doing that…"

She moved up along him again.

"If I keep doing this?"

The naughty glint had returned to her eyes.

"Yes, that."

She reached the end and moved back the other way, making him arch his back off the bed and thrust upward.

"Then what?"

He couldn't think to reply to her question. But he gripped her hips and pulled her toward him. She murmured as she slid along his body. This time when she reached the end, he lifted her slightly and moved his leaping manhood just inside of her.

She cried out as the pleasure of him pierced her and made her throb. She couldn't help rotating her hips to tease herself on his body.

This time, his upward thrust brought him deeper inside her body. She held his shoulders and pressed back, driving him home.

They began to move together.

Nigel bit off a groan and then gritted his teeth, needing to keep control. The sight of Regina's naked beauty, the feel of her honeyed warmth, the vision of her trembling breasts, the scent of her perfumed body, the sound of her muted cries of pleasure, the movement of her body as she rode along his—it all filled him with an aching for release.

Nigel reached up and spread his palm across both of her breasts, feeling both of her nipples with his fingers. Regina moaned and bucked on top of him, feeling heat spread through her breast to her center. Her throbbing became heavy and filled her entire body with unleashed longing.

She bent downward, tilting her hips so that her womanhood grazed along his rippled abdomen and her breasts along his chest, and the pleasure made her cry out.

"Nigel," she called, agonized by the need building inside of her.

"Yes, Reggie," he said, and captured her lips.

They moved as one, her body grating over his chest, his lower stomach, his manhood. The sensations singed her. She pulled her mouth away.

"Nigel, Nigel."

"Yes, Reggie, yes."

Their foreheads pressed together, he drove inside her faster and harder, responding to her call, heady with the urgency he heard in her voice.

"Nigel," she cried, "please, please."

"Reggie."

Nigel groaned. Her desire held him at the precipice, but he wanted to fulfill her need.

"Take it, Reggie. Take your pleasure from me."

Regina cried out as her muscles contracted around Nigel's thrusting member. She moaned as wave after wave of pleasure ripped through her body, blinding her to anything but the feeling of rhapsody.

Nigel felt her clench, felt her contract about him like fingers in massage. His body buckled, sending him into her in uncontrollable pulses as he felt his own release.

They wrapped their arms around each other as she collapsed on him. Nigel lowered her to his side, unsheathed himself and returned to Regina's arms.

"Everything you do drives me crazy," he said. "If I'm not careful, I'll end up in the loony bin."

He chuckled, and she elbowed him playfully.

Then Nigel got serious.

"Reggie, has it been okay being with me, us being in love? Do you still look at me and think about…what happened before?"

She reached out and touched his cheek, looking into his face.

"No. I love being with you. I don't think about what happened before."

He leaned over and kissed her mouth.

"I'm so glad. I have another question. Have you forgiven me?"

"What? Where is this coming from?"

"Have you forgiven me—for being a kid and for leaving when I should have stayed and for not being there when you lost the baby and for…everything?"

Regina sighed and thought about it so that she could answer truthfully. "Yes. Yes, I have." She hesitated, and then she added, "I need to know something, too."

"Anything."

She took a breath and looked up at the ceiling.

"Have you forgiven me for losing our child?" Tears spilled down her face.

"What?"

"I felt so ashamed that I couldn't— I wanted to tell you before, to find out before, but I couldn't. We weren't… close enough then."

"Oh, Reggie." Nigel turned to her, wrapping his arms around her. "There's nothing to forgive. It wasn't your fault. It happens."

He kissed her temples and her eyes.

"I know. I know. I guess I just had to get that off my chest. I've been holding it in for so long. I just felt…so ashamed."

"There was nothing for you to feel ashamed about. You did everything you were supposed to do."

"I know. I just couldn't help it. I couldn't help thinking it was me." Regina exhaled and shook her head to clear her mind. "I'm okay."

Nigel got up, pulling something from inside the dresser

and coming to her side of the bed, where he knelt. Regina leaned up on her elbow to meet him.

"There was a reason I needed to know the answer to those questions."

"What is it?"

"I love you with all of my heart. I'm only happy in life when I'm with you." He opened the box he'd taken from the dresser. It was his grandmother's wedding ring. "Marry me because you love me, and never think of paying me back again."

Regina sat up, bringing the covers with her. Her hand flew to her chest, and tears streamed down her face.

She took the ring from the box. It was an antique with a large diamond in the middle of a circular crest and smaller diamonds all around it. She looked at Nigel and then slipped it onto her ring finger.

She turned to face Nigel again.

"Yes. I will."

She wiped at the tears.

"But we're going to pay you back anyway—Amelie and me."

Nigel laughed, which made Regina laugh, too.

"I knew you would say that."

"Good," she said.

"I'm so happy, Reggie. I love you."

"I love you, too, Nigel."

They reached for each other at the same time, the fire reigniting between them. It had always been that way for them. She opened her arms for him, and he climbed into bed and into her embrace, their bodies coming together.

"Reggie," he said, breaking their kiss.

"Yes."

"I know that your business is just getting started, and

this might not be the best time, but when can we try for another baby, or do you still want children?"

In response, she captured his mouth with her lips, reached between them to grip him and guided him inside of her.

Nigel moaned as the wet warmth of her body surrounded his unsheathed manhood, making it spring and swell inside of her.

"Reggie, Reggie," he said, while he still had the presence of mind.

"Yes, Nigel."

"Are you sure? Are you sure you want this now?"

The answer came from her body, which clamped around him and twisted, bringing him home.

Nigel winced in exquisite anguish as Regina's heat flooded his body. He covered her mouth again, giving himself to the electricity between them.

Then Regina stopped, shaking her head to wake herself and slowing down to pull him from his reverie.

"You, what about you? Do you want this now?" she asked.

Nigel pressed his grinning face against Regina's cheek, pulled one of her nipples taut and gyrated inside of her until her hips rocked upward to ride her along his tumid crest.

"Yes, I do. Yes, I'm sure."

He drew himself out, stopping at the point he knew she liked, and made short thrusts against her until she moaned and careened her hips. But she paused again.

"You know," she said, "we're doing it backwards again—baby, marriage."

Nigel leaned up and chuckled, at least until Regina's mouth found one of his nipples and sent a quiver up his back.

When he could talk, he said, "First, this time, it's a deliberate choice. And second, I hope to be married long before it's a question in anybody's mind."

Regina turned Nigel on his side and started to get up, but he held her back.

"Where are you going?"

"I have to start planning a wedding."

Nigel laughed, and then she did, too.

"We can start that tomorrow."

"We better, at the rate we're going."

His was still wedged deep inside her body and turned her onto her back again. He put his hands beneath her shoulders and slowly dove deeper inside of her. She pressed her fingers into his back and pivoted along his thrust. Their lips found one another, and their bodies moved together.

They were going to make it a long night.

* * * * *

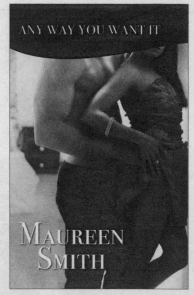

A classic novel in the bestselling Hideaway series!

NATIONAL BESTSELLING AUTHOR

ROCHELLE ALERS

Homecoming

Reporter Dana Nichols has come home to Mississippi determined to uncover the truth behind her parents' long-ago murder-suicide tragedy and finally clear her family name. The last thing she expects is her instant attraction to handsome, dedicated doctor Tyler Cole. As she and Tyler search for answers, they end up walking a dangerous line between trust and uncertainty that will put their future love at stake….

"Homecoming is the latest in Ms. Alers' Hideaway series, and boy, what an intense installment it's proven to be!"
— *RT Book Reviews* on *Homecoming*

Available December 2012 wherever books are sold!

REQUEST YOUR FREE BOOKS!

2 FREE NOVELS
PLUS 2 *FREE GIFTS!*

KIMANI™ ROMANCE

Love's ultimate destination!

YES! Please send me 2 FREE Kimani™ Romance novels and my 2 FREE gifts (gifts are worth about $10). After receiving them, if I don't wish to receive any more books, I can return the shipping statement marked "cancel." If I don't cancel, I will receive 4 brand-new novels every month and be billed just $4.94 per book in the U.S. or $5.49 per book in Canada. That's a savings of at least 21% off the cover price. It's quite a bargain! Shipping and handling is just 50¢ per book in the U.S. and 75¢ per book in Canada.* I understand that accepting the 2 free books and gifts places me under no obligation to buy anything. I can always return a shipment and cancel at any time. Even if I never buy another book, the two free books and gifts are mine to keep forever.

168/368 XDN FVUK

Name	(PLEASE PRINT)
Address	Apt. #
City	State/Prov.	Zip/Postal Code

Signature (if under 18, a parent or guardian must sign)

Mail to the Harlequin® Reader Service:
IN U.S.A.: P.O. Box 1867, Buffalo, NY 14240-1867
IN CANADA: P.O. Box 609, Fort Erie, Ontario L2A 5X3

Want to try two free books from another line?
Call 1-800-873-8635 or visit www.ReaderService.com.

* Terms and prices subject to change without notice. Prices do not include applicable taxes. Sales tax applicable in N.Y. Canadian residents will be charged applicable taxes. Offer not valid in Quebec. This offer is limited to one order per household. Not valid for current subscribers to Kimani Romance books. All orders subject to credit approval. Credit or debit balances in a customer's account(s) may be offset by any other outstanding balance owed by or to the customer. Please allow 4 to 6 weeks for delivery. Offer available while quantities last.

Your Privacy—The Harlequin® Reader Service is committed to protecting your privacy. Our Privacy Policy is available online at www.ReaderService.com or upon request from the Harlequin Reader Service.

We make a portion of our mailing list available to reputable third parties that offer products we believe may interest you. If you prefer that we not exchange your name with third parties, or if you wish to clarify or modify your communication preferences, please visit us at www.ReaderService.com/consumerschoice or write to us at Harlequin Reader Service Preference Service, P.O. Box 9062, Buffalo, NY 14269. Include your complete name and address.

KROM13

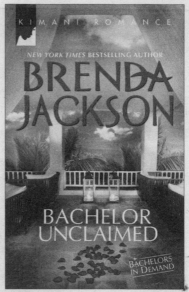